Sherlock Holmes and the Ripper File

Antony James

Edited by
Lindsay Siviter

Breese Books

THE Publisher for Quality Murder Mystery Books &
Home to the Breese Books Sherlock Holmes Collection

First published in 2023 by
Breese Books
for Baker Street Studios Ltd and
The Irregular Special Press
Endeavour House
170 Woodland Road, Sawston
Cambridge, CB22 3DX, UK

ISBN: 978-1-901091-90-8

Cover Picture: *A Suspicious Character* from The *Illustrated London News*, 13th October
1888. Drawing of a man with a pulled-up collar and pulled-down hat being watched
by two well-dressed men (who resemble Sherlock Holmes and Dr. John Watson).

Typeset in 8/11/20pt Palatino

Contents

Introduction 5

The Question 7

Return to London 13

The Suspects 19

Whitechapel 33

Mary Ann 'Polly' Nichols 43

Annie Chapman 53

Elizabeth Stride 63

Catherine Eddowes 69

The Writing on the Wall 79

Mary Kelly 89

The Alpha 99

... And Omega 109

Denouement 121

Photographic Appendix 135

Acknowledgements, References & Further Reading 157

Introduction

Since 1888 the gruesome crimes of Jack the Ripper have been a never-ending source of fascination to generations of professional, amateur, and armchair detectives. What is more, those murders are no nearer being solved today as they were back in Victorian times – or are they?

Bringing together a wealth of research materials along with new ideas, J. P. Sperati in his book *In the Footsteps of Jack the Ripper*[1] meticulously investigated those dark deeds – the so-called canonical 5 murders plus a further 8 cases – which constituted the complete Whitechapel Murders spanning the years 1888-1891. Sperati treated each case from a historical context and included extra information highlighting additional points of interest. After examining a number of known suspects, all of which he subsequently eliminated, Sperati came to a unique conclusion regarding the true identity of the serial killer known to millions as Jack the Ripper.

This book, set in 1908, is based upon that definitive study, but here the story is told through the eyes of Sherlock Holmes, or rather Dr. John Watson for it is on a visit to see the retired consulting detective that Watson asks Holmes whether his services were ever called upon by Scotland Yard twenty years

---

[1] Sperati, J. P., *In the Footsteps of Jack the Ripper*, 208 pages, Irregular Special Press, (2021), ISBN: 978-1-909091-78-6.

earlier. It transpires that Holmes was indeed instrumental in stopping the Ripper, but that he is unwilling to divulge the identity of the serial killer since he is still sworn to secrecy. However, he challenges Watson to take a retrospective look at the case using all the available information from the time which he had gathered and bound into a Ripper File. With Holmes acting as guide they visit the locations of the murders where clues are still to be found nearly two decades later.

It is most certainly a case of *solvitur ambulando*, but does Watson come to the same conclusion as Holmes did back in the day? Read on and all will be revealed in a text (with appropriate illustrations indicated by bold square brackets e.g. [1]) which should be a must for all those who wish to follow in the footsteps of Jack the Ripper, as well as those just interested in the history of London's East End.

Chapter One

The Question

"May I ask you a question, Holmes? There is something that has been bothering me for a little while ..."

"Just the one thing?" interrupted my friend, with a wry smile.

He was in good humour this evening, perhaps, I hoped, because I was visiting him at his cottage near Seaford on the Sussex Downs for the first time since he had retired officially and taken up residence there. As one grows older it is strange how quickly time passes. There always seems to be so many mundane things to occupy one's time rather than those which are of real importance. For my part I could not believe that Holmes had ceased work some five years ago in 1903, having developed his latest interest in beekeeping (as was evidenced by several hives in his back garden) over the last two years while I, his best and perhaps only friend, had continued in general practice back in the smoke-filled capital.

Long had I wished to come and visit, and my new wife had even encouraged it, saying that it would do me good to have a break by the sea and get away from all those troublesome patients for whom I seemed to be endlessly on call. She knew that I missed Holmes and our adventures together, and that he probably felt the same way about me, although being Holmes he would never admit to it. And now, but only after Mycroft, Holmes's elder brother, had confided in me that he sensed that

Sherlock might be suffering one of his periods of mental anguish due to the lack of anything to occupy his mind fully, I had finally grasped the nettle and dispatched myself by train that fine day, just as the leaves on the trees were showing signs of changing colour, heralding autumn. The journey from Victoria station had been a pleasant one. Thankfully, only a single change of trains at Lewes, unlike the last time I was in this part of the country when Holmes was evading the clutches of a certain mathematics professor who was pursuing him to the Continent, and to that fateful meeting at the Reichenbach Falls. On that occasion we had changed trains at Canterbury and subsequently made for the boat at Newhaven, only about five miles distant from where Holmes was now ensconced in a small, but quite adequate, dwelling set back from those famous white cliffs in a sheltered position ideal for his beloved bees.

"My question involves something which you have never mentioned to me, but about which I feel sure you must have knowledge."

"Continue," said he, helping himself to another brandy from the decanter on the side table.

"Well, cast your mind back to early in your career and the case which I published under the title of *A Scandal in Bohemia*."

"Come, Watson, you are being far too diplomatic as you know full well that I might not take kindly to you mentioning the name Irene Adler to me, the lady with whom I was hopelessly in love ... at least according to your account in *The Strand Magazine*."

"Perhaps I did exaggerate a little, but you must allow me some poetic license in these matters ..."

"Certainly not. You infuriated me at the time by the mere suggestion that I felt any kind of romantic emotion for her when, the truth is, I only admired her for her intellect, and the fact that she saw through my plans with such ease."

"And the photograph of her that I note you still keep on the mantlepiece?" said I, pointing in the direction of a prominently placed framed image, which occupied pride of place above the fireplace.

"A reminder only, Watson ... a reminder never to underestimate a woman again."

I felt slightly uneasy now as to the direction in which the conversation was heading, so to gain time I, too, helped myself to a second brandy while I tried to think of something to say to break the tension that I had just created. I had no need, for Holmes, in that insufferable way of his, was ahead of my thoughts all the time.

"Anyway, it is not that case which concerns you, is it? So, let me think ... yes, the Bohemian affair took place in early 1888, so I do believe that you wish to ask me about events in the late summer and autumn of that year ... am I not correct?"

"As usual, Holmes, you are. According to my notes, there were no other cases with which you were involved during that period, and yet between August and November that year London was gripped by terror ..."

"By the so-called Whitechapel murders, which have long been attributed as the work of Jack the Ripper, and you want to know if I was ever consulted."

"Well, they were never solved."

"And what makes you think that?"

"It was widely covered in the press, don't forget. The papers were very critical of the police for despite numerous arrests, none were to result in a conviction."

"Oh, and you believe every little thing you read do you, Watson?"

"Well, not every little thing, but on this occasion they all spoke as one, and there were no official statements as to the Ripper being unmasked were there? Only endless suspects and speculation."

"And yet after the murder of Mary Jane Kelly in the November the atrocities purportedly stopped ... how do you explain that, my friend?"

"Are you trying to tell me that there was some kind of an arrest unknown to the public ... a conspiracy within the police, or worse still within government, Holmes?"

"What I can tell you for sure is that two of the highest-ranking persons involved with the investigation, Assistant

Chief Constable Melville Macnaghten and Assistant Commissioner Robert Anderson, both thought that they knew the identity of Jack the Ripper, and gave instructions for that person to be removed from society."

"Removed?"

"Yes, the suspect in question was a Polish Jew with the surname Kosminski, although there is some ambiguity over the spelling of his name and exact identity. He lived in Whitechapel, worked as a barber and hairdresser, and was said to have a hatred of all women, especially prostitutes."

"Well, it certainly sounds as if the killer could have been a paranoid schizophrenic, and a barber like Kosminski would have had the tools for the job close at hand, but was there any actual evidence that this man was the Ripper?"

"Only that an unnamed witness positively identified him as such, but then apparently refused to testify once they realised that Kosminski was a fellow Jew."

"You said removed ..."

"Yes, Kosminski was arrested and initially placed in the Colney Hatch Asylum, but later in April 1894 was moved to the one at Leavesden where the fellow has remained ever since."

"Were you that witness by any chance, Holmes?"

"Goodness gracious, no, Watson. I had my thoughts in a completely different direction, and in any case I am not, as you well know, Jewish."

"So, you don't think that this Kosminski was the Ripper then?"

"He might have been."

"What do you mean by that?"

"No more or less than what I just said ... he might have been the Ripper, though he was not the person I suspected."

"So, did you solve the case by proving that it was your suspect, Holmes?" I retorted, becoming somewhat tetchy at the lack of definitive answers from my friend.

"I might have done."

"For God's sake, Holmes, you either solved it, or you didn't."

"It's not quite as easy as all that for although I did identify the person I believed to be the murderer, I was never to know if my information bore fruit, only that soon after my intervention the killings ceased."

"That is very unlike you not to follow through on a case to the very end."

"Indeed, Watson, but this was no ordinary case. For a start I was not brought in until after the first four murders had been committed, and then my involvement was through Mycroft and the Home Secretary only. I was rather restricted and not allowed to speak with any of the suspects, or the police officers on the case, though I was given access to endless reports."

"That sounds pretty intolerable to me, Holmes."

"It was, but then I was only asked to give an opinion as to the type of person that could carry out such atrocities, not to name the actual killer."

"And that you did?"

"Yes."

"Well don't hold back now, it's twenty years since those dark days ... surely you can tell me who you thought it was at the time?"

Holmes finished the last mouthful of his brandy, and then, while considering my request, decided to putter around filling his pipe for what seemed like an eternity. At long last, following the successful lighting of the briar, he answered.

"I suspect that I am still bound by the Official Secrets Act of 1889, but it would be very satisfying if, given the same evidence to which I was privy, you could come up with the same solution as I. That way no confidences would be betrayed."

That idea piqued my interest since Holmes had never been particularly complimentary about my own skills of observation, or analytical reasoning for that matter.

"I accept. When and where do I start?"

"Watson, let me tell you something that may surprise you ... people from inland towns and cities often think that those of us who are fortunate enough to live by the sea are in a permanent state of holiday and as such have no need of a break ourselves. That is a fallacy, for nothing could be further from the truth. I have been here for several years now and I am in desperate need of a return to London, a city that has a better variety of landscapes on offer than any coastline can match. So, as it is getting late let me propose that you stay here tonight, and then tomorrow after breakfast we will depart for London together, where I will act as your guide to those locations where the crimes took place. How does that suit you, Watson?"

"Very well ... very well, indeed, Holmes."

Chapter Two

Return to London

Gone were the days when I could expect a tap on my shoulder at first light and hear those familiar words 'Quick, the game's afoot, Watson', for now the retired Holmes approached life in a more leisurely fashion. The following morning, we breakfasted together at nine-thirty before making for the train at Seaford, which according to Bradshaw's departed a little after eleven. When I tried to hurry him along, he merely remarked that there was no great urgency since the trail had been cold for two decades, and that we had no need to arrive in Whitechapel until after dark in order that the conditions should replicate those at the times of the various murders as closely as possible.

Having purchased our tickets at the railway station, we had little trouble in finding a compartment to ourselves, given that we were travelling outside of the busiest periods. Holmes was content to simply stare out of the window at the changing landscape, while I was full of questions. Seeing my obvious agitation at the silence between us he finally took pity upon me.

"So, Watson, although as a medical man you will have had no formal training into the psychology of persons like our friend Jack the Ripper, as my companion on numerous adventures I am sure that you will have thoughts on the possible motivations of such a man."

"A good question, Holmes." I paused, trying to collect my thoughts into some sort of order.

"I know, Watson, otherwise I would not have asked it in the first place, would I?" He smiled.

The fact that Holmes was in such a playful mood told me that he was already relishing the thought of what was yet to come. Perhaps, I surmised, rather uncharitably, he was merely looking forward to showing me just how feeble my own deductions might be in relation to his own. However, I hoped that I could give him a good run for his money, for I had a trick up my sleeve that he could know nothing about.

"To a layperson, multiple murderers, such as Jack the Ripper, may seem to be devoid of any logic, meaning, or motivation. However, in the background there will always be a trigger. If you can discover that trigger you will be well on the way to capturing the fiend."

"Excellent, Watson, but what sort of persons become such fiends in the first instance?"

"In the main they will be insecure individuals who are compelled to kill due to some morbid fear of rejection. Often this relates to a childhood experience where they were rejected by their mother, or father ... or perhaps both. It may seem strange to comprehend but most do not derive any pleasure from their terrible deeds, though they do commit them because they want to. The victims are usually chosen based on availability, vulnerability, and desirability."

"I agree with your synopsis, Watson, but in the specific instance of the Ripper what do you suggest was that trigger, as you so aptly put it?"

"The most obvious one would be anger, which could manifest itself towards a certain subgroup of people such as Jews or prostitutes for example."

"That would certainly be true for Kosminski and most likely for any other Ripper suspect given that all the women were prostitutes. As you will discover later, there may have been a Jewish element as well to the killings, though my own view is that this was a red herring."

"Another motivation might be criminal enterprise whereby through their acts the killer gains respect within their circle. And then there is pure financial gain as with, for example, multiple killings that involve a fraud of some kind. I would submit that neither of these are relevant to the Ripper."

"Quite so, Watson. Do continue."

"Ideology is also a powerful whip for some to take action. This could relate to gender, some religious, or even ethnic belief."

"You mean that somebody like the Ripper might believe that all those who are of Chinese descent, as an example, might need to be eradicated?"

"Monstrous I know, but there are those who think like that, which is how wars may begin. I saw it first hand in some of the soldiers while I was in Afghanistan ... men who on arrival were quite sober in thought change when faced with the horrors of such a bloody campaign. At Maiwand we were outnumbered ten to one, and lost nearly half our number ... that can turn a man into a savage wanting revenge at any cost for fallen comrades. "

"Yes, I see. It might be relevant to the Ripper if his ideology was the elimination of all prostitutes, but, somehow, I think not."

"I agree, Holmes. It is more likely that he gets a feeling of exhilaration while performing his mutilations."

"And that he obtains some sort of power from what he does as well. Do you think that this could also be a sexual act, Watson?"

"Sometimes, but in such cases I believe that the motive is desire, but not necessarily physical contact."

"Well, that scenario would also fit the Ripper since although there was no evidence that any of the women had been violated in that way, there was most certainly a desire I would say."

"Finally, there could be a deep psychosis involved, in which case the Ripper simply could not help himself due to a severe mental illness which might involve hallucinations, paranoia, or bizarre delusions."

"So, apart from criminal enterprise and financial gain, the killings could have been triggered by a number of things."

Holmes laughed before continuing.

"I think that now you are beginning to understand that this case was more complex than at first you thought. Not quite as simple as a robbery where there is a clear motive and where logic can be used to track down the culprit. I have often said that the perfect crime is the one committed on the spur of the moment without motive, and with the least fuss. If somebody takes a gun and shoots a complete stranger at midnight in the absence of witnesses, then he or she is likely never to be caught. It was only because the Ripper continued with his atrocities that I was able to help the authorities."

"You said last night that you only thought that you had identified the Ripper ..."

"Quite so," interrupted Holmes.

"Well, suppose just for a moment that you were wrong, and if so do you have any theories as to why the killings ceased so suddenly?"

"You are full of questions this morning, Watson. I do believe that the sea air and a solid night's sleep has done you the power of good."

"The question remains, Holmes. What if you were wrong?"

"Looking at it logically there are several possibilities. First, he or she might have died, or for some reason could not continue. This might be because of accidental death, through ill health, suicide, death by natural causes, or even because they were murdered by somebody else who came to know of their identity."

"Do you think any of these explanations likely, Holmes?"

"Maybe, but not probable I grant you. Equally they might have ended the killings of their own accord if they had achieved their aim, or had been cured."

"I do not subscribe to that idea, Holmes. In my limited experience the killer continues on until they are caught ... there is no concept that they ever complete their mission as there will always be another person deserving their attention, and as for being cured ..."

"Yes, I agree with you, Watson, so let's discard that line of thought as well. However, it is possible that they may have travelled elsewhere to continue their work. There were quite credible theories at the time that the Ripper went to the United States, and, indeed, was an American. Unfortunately, the person most often cited in that regard is my namesake, Henry Howard Holmes, who is generally regarded as the first American multiple killer. He confessed to the murder of over twenty persons, though the true number may have been ten times that, at his infamous 'murder castle' of a hotel in Chicago, Illinois. There is some circumstantial evidence that he was here in London at the time of the Whitechapel murders. But I assure you that he was not the Ripper for his trigger was most certainly money. He would seduce women, become engaged to them, murder them, and then claim their life savings. He didn't stop there either for he also made all his employees take out life insurance policies with him as the sole beneficiary."

"Are you not forgetting a final alternative fate of the Ripper, Holmes? He could have been arrested and jailed for some other crime and so taken off the streets ... or placed in an asylum, with or without a trial."

"I was wondering if you were going to bring up the fate of Kosminski again, Watson. You are, of course, correct and your point is well taken. You might not realise it, but you are already making good progress in your investigation."

So enraptured with our conversation had I been that it was only now that I glanced out of the carriage window to be greeted with familiar rows of terraced houses lining the multiple tracks as we snaked through South London. Soon we would be crossing Victoria Bridge and approaching journey's end.

"In a few minutes we will be at the terminus. I suggest we take some lunch at the Grosvenor, and then proceed to Whitechapel."

"No, Baker Street, Watson."

"Baker Street, Holmes?"

"Yes, Watson. Although I no longer reside there, Mrs. Hudson has been kind enough to invite us both for lunch. I telephoned her first thing this morning while you were still asleep ... she was delighted at the prospect, I assure you."

"Really, I thought that she would find herself discombobulated at the thought of your return at such short notice ..."

"Not at all, Watson. I always feared that you never really understood our landlady as I did. There is also a more practical reason for our visit since I still store some boxes of my papers in the basement, and in one of them are my original notes on the investigation, which I gathered together in what I call my Ripper File. You will be most welcome to examine it as the contents will be instructive in your investigation."

Chapter Three

The Suspects

Despite the fact that at times the relationship between Holmes and Mrs. Hudson had been a strained one, entirely I might add because of the former's habits, the welcome received from our old landlady was more like that reserved for a close relative. No one upon seeing them now could ever imagine that on more than one occasion she had referred to him as being the 'worst tenant in London', an epithet fully justified due to his constant malodorous chemical experiments, callers at all hours of the day and night, and the occasional report of a gun firing into the wall (which in one instance formed the patriotic letters 'VR'). All that was forgotten now as we were shown into her ground floor parlour and offered drinks prior to a substantial late lunch served in her small dining room toward the back of her rooms at 221A Baker Street. Over coffee, back in the parlour, I gave her some medical advice concerning her hips which had been giving her pain for some months, while Holmes disappeared to the basement to seek out the relevant papers he had left there when he had officially retired. He returned triumphant with what appeared to be one of his commonplace books held aloft. It was, in fact, his Ripper File.

"Have a look at this, Watson," he commanded, as he placed it on the table next to me.

So eager was I to take a look that I very nearly knocked over the coffee pot as I took charge of the volume. It was much

19

slimmer than I had expected, and comprised of handwritten notes beside cuttings from a whole variety of different sources.

"So, this is it," I muttered as I turned the pages in anticipation.

"It is, Watson, and everything you need to solve the murders is contained within."

I noticed that many column inches were scored through in red, while other paragraphs had question marks next to them and occasionally the word 'check' along with a corresponding note if verification had been completed. The section that interested me most was the one headed 'Suspects', which contained a dozen names.

"And which one of the suspects in your list did it turn out to be, Holmes?" said I, without any great expectation of receiving a direct response, but I was wrong on this occasion.

"None of them, Watson."

"And why not? I recognise most of the names from coverage in the newspapers at the time. Didn't the first on your list, Dr. Cream [1], actually confess to being the Ripper?"

"Indeed, he did, but I regard him as a very doubtful suspect, albeit he was most certainly responsible for several murders. The problem is that his *modus operandi* was always poison, strychnine to be precise, and his motive financial gain. He certainly did nothing to enhance the reputation of doctors, and should have been struck off more than once. He specialised in illegal abortions, which he performed in Canada, the United States and right here in London. He was eventually caught, put to trial, and sentenced to death by hanging. On the day in question in November 1892 his last words at the gallows were allegedly 'I am Jack the ...' with the final word being interrupted by the noose tightening as he dropped to his death."

"Do you think that he just wanted the notoriety, Holmes?"

"Undoubtedly. Remind me, who is next on the list?"

"Montague John Druitt [2]."

"Ah, yes ... he was certainly a prime suspect at the time, at least according to the Assistant Chief Constable Melville Macnaghten."

"It says here that he was born in 1857 and was a Winchester and Oxford man, originally studying to become a doctor, but ended up a barrister. Not a meteoric career progression since it took him until 1885 to be called to the bar at the Inner Temple."

"Quite so, Watson ... I suspect that he was somewhat mediocre in all things given that he also had to take a position as an assistant schoolmaster at George Valentine's boarding school in Blackheath."

"I know that place, I've played rugby against that prestigious establishment, Holmes ... I might even have come into contact with Druitt since it says here that he was both a cricketer and a rugby player of some note, but I just cannot imagine a school teacher being the Ripper." I read on. "Ah, now I see why he was a suspect ... he was dismissed from his position at the school on the thirtieth of November 1888 and committed suicide by drowning shortly afterwards, leaving a letter in which he referred to his insane mother." I paused again while I read the relevant note in the margin. "'Since Friday last, I felt I was going to be like Mother and the best thing for me was to die'. Druitt's body was recovered from the Thames on the thirty-first of December 1888, and investigation by the police revealed that he had no alibi at the time of any of the murders. Suspicious indeed."

"It might interest you to know, Watson, that I, too, had no alibi for any for the murders, but that does not make me a suspect! Druitt had no connections to the East End, save that his cousin Lionel worked in the Minories as a doctor, and it is just happenstance that the murders stopped immediately after his death."

"There is a further note here that he was, as you put it, 'insane' and 'derived pleasure from extreme violence' ... surely that makes him a suspect?"

"I did, of course, investigate and as well as this dark side to his character he was a lifelong bachelor and his dismissal as a schoolmaster was due to an unsupported suspicion of pederasty within Valentine's."

"Good God, Holmes ... who would ever believe that such things could go on in a boarding school?"

"Maybe not at the one where you were educated, but you would be surprised, my friend ... but at least it clears him of being the Ripper since, if the allegations were true, women would not figure greatly in his thoughts. He was certainly a tormented individual, but not our killer. Next."

I turned the page to be confronted with the image of a familiar figure in Victorian society.

"Ah, yes the Royal conspiracy theory[1] is that Prince Albert Victor Christian Edward [3] had been driven insane after contracting syphilis and as a result became Jack the Ripper, exacting revenge on the unfortunates of Whitechapel."

"Absolute poppycock, Watson. In the first place Prince Eddy, as he was known to most, it can be proved beyond reasonable doubt was as far away as Grosmont in Yorkshire, in York itself, Abergeldie in Scotland, and on the Sandringham estate in Norfolk at the time of four of the murders. The only points against him are that he was an enthusiastic deer-hunter and so knew about butchery, and that he had an eye for the ladies. What you may have read in the newspapers about there being a Royal cover up, and him being placed in asylum at Sandringham is all conjecture. To my certain knowledge there has never been an asylum at Sandringham, private or otherwise. The only thing known for sure is that he died in 1892."

"Not so fast, Holmes. Were there not other suspicions at the time concerning Prince Eddy? Was it not proposed that he had sired a child with one of the unfortunates in Whitechapel who was a Catholic? Now that would be worth covering up, and what is more with his status the deed would almost certainly be done by others under the instructions of the authorities to avoid such a scandal."

"Yes, you are, of course, correct, but only in as far as that there were rumours. According to those rumours it was a coachman named John Netley who drove Sir William Gull [4] about the East End, with that eminent Royal physician being charged with the task committing those atrocities ... and

---

[1] Holmes is ahead of the times here since this theory was not suggested until the 1970s.

behind it all were the Freemasons, that secretive society of brethren, trying their best to save the Royal family from possible blackmail.[2]"

"Well, it is possible … as you say they are a secret society with the highest connections …"

At this point Holmes held up his hand to stop me saying anything further.

"No, Watson. They are not a secret society, but a society with secrets, and the whole idea of Sir William going about cutting up young ladies in the small hours is preposterous. He may have had the technical knowledge, but I very much doubt that he was physically capable of doing anything of that sort given that he was seventy-one at the time, in poor health, and was to die just over a year later following a stroke. In addition he was not even in London at the time of the killings and was not even a Freemason … case closed I think, Watson."

The list of suspects was being whittled down very quickly.

"I see that you did consider our friend Aaron Kosminski at some length."

"Only because Assistant Chief Constable Melville Macnaghten [5] and the Assistant Commissioner Robert Anderson [6] were convinced of his guilt and directed me to investigate further."

"According to the note you made at the time it seems that Anderson said that 'the only person who ever had a good view of the murderer at once identified him, but when he learned that the suspect was a fellow-Jew he declined to swear to him'. Pretty damning evidence, I would say."

"We did discuss him yesterday, and it is possible that he was the Ripper, but there were too many inconsistencies to be positive. For instance, while in the asylum at Colney Hatch Kosminski was described as being 'harmless' with his only misdemeanours being to threaten a woman, who may have been his sister, with a knife and brandishing a chair at an asylum assistant. There is even reason to think that it may have been a case of mistaken identity since in the same asylum was

---

[2] This theory actually originated in the 1970s reaching a height of popularity in Stephen Knight's 1976 book *Jack the Ripper: The Final Solution*.

another Polish Jew, a bootmaker, who was violent and who had to be restrained. He went by the name of Aaron Davis Cohen, but there has been speculation that he was actually Nathan Kaminsky. It would not be the first time that the police mixed up similar names."

"I see the problem. The only evidence comes from this unidentified witness who refused to testify, and the fact that the killings stopped once Kosminski was off the streets."

I returned to the Ripper File and the next suspect.

"James Maybrick [7] ... I do not recognise that name. Why is he included in your list?"

"He shouldn't be by rights as he was a murder victim himself in May 1889."

"But not by the Ripper then?"

"No, he almost certainly killed by his wife who poisoned him with arsenic. In fact, he was a womaniser and so it is unlikely that he would take to murdering the unfortunates. The sole reason he is included in the list is that sometime afterward a diary purporting to be his appeared in which the writer confesses that he is Jack the Ripper. As you know, Watson, I am somewhat an expert on handwriting and having examined it at length I am convinced that the penmanship is not representative of other samples of Maybrick's hand."

"So as with Cream he, or somebody else, just wanted him to have the notoriety," I stated with some confidence.

"Indeed, but there is another string to this bow in that some time later a pocket watch was found upon which 'J. Maybrick' was scratched on the inside cover, but more damningly next to that name were the words 'I am Jack' and the initials of the five victims."

"A fake inscription no doubt," I interjected.

"If so, it was a very well executed fraud as I must confess that I could not discount it, although I am certain in my mind that must be the case as there is nothing else that presents itself to give Maybrick either motive, opportunity or means, despite the fact that it transpired that he had a secret wife and family living in Whitechapel at the time. He is not our man, Watson, and nor is Michael Ostrog [8] who you will also find on the list of suspects I investigated."

Indeed, his name was there on the following page.

"It says here that he was another of those identified by Melville Macnaghten as being of great interest, and like our friend Kosminski was also detained in an asylum without trial, although in his case he was later released to subsequently disappear from all public records from 1904 onwards."

"No great loss to the world, Watson, as Ostrog was a homicidal maniac, with his *modus operandi* being to prey on women for money ... he had no hatred of women himself, quite the opposite, and so would not have been disposed to ripping them open like an animal carcass. Russian by birth, possibly a doctor, but most certainly a conman, confidence trickster and thief. He had over twenty aliases and spent more than one spell in prison. However, Ostrog is not the Ripper given that his physical appearance in no way fitted that given by any of the witnesses. He was much too tall for a start."

"Is that a reason to discount him, Holmes? As we both well know witness descriptions can be very unreliable to say the least, and you yourself when in disguise can become any person you wish to portray whether tall or short."

"Normally that would be a valid point, but not in this case as there is some compelling evidence suggesting that he was in a French prison at the time of at least one of the murders."

"Well then, this is a waste of time," said I closing the book and placing it back on the table, getting ever more despondent as each suspect was eliminated.

"Quite the reverse, I assure you. In science every experiment has a value even if it is a negative result, or not the outcome you expect. Here being able to eliminate a person is also of value and helps focus the mind towards the truth, and hopefully the perpetrator in time."

"Yes, you are correct, most assuredly, but there are just so many suspects to consider in this case."

"You do not know the half of it, Watson. The police were swamped with concerned citizens trying to help ... there were literally hundreds of people put under suspicion in this way, many for no better reason than that they had an evil look about them, or used a knife in their work. I genuinely had pity for the police in this instance since they were duty-bound to sift through every lead, whereas I could concentrate on just a handful of suspects. Now, what are your views on the artist Walter Sickert[3] **[9]** ... you will find him lurking there somewhere?"

I took the Ripper File back in hand and opened it at the same page from which I had previously been reading, but there was no mention of Sickert. I turned the pages furiously until I found him, at which juncture I noted something different about his entry.

"Ah, I deduce that he wasn't a suspect at the time, Holmes."

"Excellent, you are coming along nicely after all those years under my tuition ... but what makes you say that?"

"For a start there are no contemporary newspaper cuttings about him, and your handwritten notes are much fresher upon the page, plus the rather obvious fact that he is the last person on your list, being squeezed in between your suspects section and the next. Hence, he was somewhat of an after-thought and added much later."

"Pray continue, Watson."

"All it says here is that he had an 'unhealthy interest in Jack the Ripper' to the extent that he even produced a painting entitled *Jack the Ripper's Bedroom*. This exhibited his gullibility since it was his landlady that told him that her previous lodger had been the infamous multiple murderer."

"Do you not know something else about the man, Watson? Something that you may have read in the press more recently?"

I racked my brain, and soon enough it came to me.

"The Camden Town murder last year ... what was the name of the prostitute in question? Emily Dimmock ... had her throat cut while asleep. But the police had their man for that, albeit the guileful barrister got him off ... surely it wasn't Sickert in the dock, was it?"

---

[3] The name of Walter Sickert really became associated with the Whitechapel Murders in the 1970s and culminated in the Patricia Cornwell 2002 book *Portrait of a Killer: Jack the Ripper – Case Closed.*

"The man you are thinking of is Robert Wood, a fellow artist who was almost certainly not the murderer, but that is not important here."

"So why mention it?"

"Because my dear Watson, since then our friend Sickert has made a number of paintings and drawings, all quite graphic, about the Camden Town murder. He is obsessed with such crimes, but not to the extent of perpetrating them himself, and for that reason he is not the Ripper."

"What on earth causes somebody like Sickert to have such a fascination with the macabre?"

"Unknown, even to the best of psychologists, but it is just possible that in this specific case that it is due to the fact that he had what is termed 'a congenital anomality of the male anatomy' which might help explain his unnatural interest with prostitutes and their murder. However, the one point you have failed to note is that Sickert is still alive, and yet there have been no further murders of such ferocity as those attributed to the Ripper ... do you not think it likely that if the Ripper were still alive and at large that he would not be committing more such atrocities until eventually caught?"

"Let us move on then? This fellow Alexander Pedachenko sounds interesting ... a member of the Russian secret police sent to discredit the Czarist Metropolitan Police by showing how incompetent they are at solving crimes. Sounds a little far-fetched, Holmes, and why would our police be considered Czarist in the first place?"

"Czarists for tolerating the presence of emigrant dissidents and anarchists in the East End, Watson."

"It gets even better when you say that he had a female accomplice who would first engage the unfortunate women in conversation while he then approached from behind and attacked them. If there is any truth in any of this why did the killings stop?"

"Because Pedachenko had been successful in completing his mission when Commissioner Sir Charles Warren was forced to resign. Pedachenko was recalled to Moscow, where by chance he was subsequently arrested and placed in an asylum after he murdered a woman in Petrograd."

"And you investigated him, Holmes?"

"Superficially my dear Watson, for it transpired that Pedachenko might not have been his true identity. Some sources say that he was actually Vassily Konovalov, or Count Andrey Luiskovo."

"And what sources might these be with such a fanciful tale to tell?"

"An excellent question, Watson. The original source for this suspect came from a document entitled *Great Russian Criminals* that was authored by none other than Grigori Rasputin ... need I say more?"

"No, you need not. I assume that there is no evidence that this person ever existed and that the whole thing was probably a work of fiction invented by the Russian government in order to simply confuse and misinform."

"You should never assume, Watson, but in this instance you are correct in your deductions."

I scanned the text and noted just three names left to consider; Dr. Stanley, Dr. Frances Tumblety [10], and Joseph Barnett [11].

"Doctors do seem to make good suspects," I murmured, almost to myself.

"That should be of no surprise to you, Watson. After all we have met a bad doctor or two in our time, haven't we?"

"Indeed, who could ever forget Dr. Grimesby Roylott of Stoke Moran and that dreadful Speckled Band affair," I rejoined.

"As I think I said at the time, and repeat here, when doctors are inclined to go wrong, they make the first of criminals ... they have the means and can create the opportunity without being even suspected due their elevated position within society."

"So, what of this Dr. Stanley ... you have written almost nothing in your file about him save that he was a cancer specialist in London and had the motive of revenge following the death of his son, who had contracted syphilis from an unfortunate in Whitechapel. The woman in question was Mary Kelly, the last of the Ripper's victims, who Stanley tracked down, along with several of her friends, before fleeing to Buenos Aires. Surely you did not have to travel to Argentina, Holmes?"

"There was no need since there is no record of a Dr. Stanley ever existing. Just like Pedachenko he is the creation of some furtive imagination."

"Was this Frances Tumblety also a figment of somebody's imagination?"

"I wish that he were, Watson, but the gentleman in question has a well-chronicled life of crime. He was a charlatan doctor born in Ireland, but operating for much of his life in Canada and the United States where he portrayed himself as an Indian herbalist. He hated all women, especially prostitutes, and blamed his misogyny on his failed marriage to one. Among his eccentricities, he collected uteruses which he displayed in glass jars and would show to his male friends."

I gasped at this atrocious behaviour. "Bizarre indeed, but is there evidence that he was in London at the time of the Whitechapel murders?"

"It is known that he visited Europe several times and for a while practiced in Liverpool until one of his patients died … after that he fled to London. It is not known for certain if he was a resident in the East End during the summer of 1888, but he was arrested by the Metropolitan Police on the 7th November that year on charges of gross indecency of a homosexual nature."

"What happened next?"

"He was granted bail and fled back to America via France, and although he was placed under surveillance he could not be sent back to England for trial as no treaty existed between our two countries at that time. Interestingly, he gave an interview to a newspaper reporter working for *New York World* in 1889 in which he admitted to being in the East End during the time of the murders. However, it makes little difference as physically he did not fit the description given by any of the witnesses, and even more importantly he was in custody awaiting his bail hearing on the night that Mary Kelly was murdered."

"That just leaves Joseph Barnett."

"At last, a credible suspect. He was the lover of Mary Kelly, and it is speculated that he so hated the thought of her turning to prostitution after he had lost his job at Billingsgate market that he turned to murdering other unfortunates in an attempt at frightening his girlfriend away from that trade."

"His motive sounds a little far-fetched, but as a former fish porter he would certainly be proficient with a knife, even if not human anatomy."

"True, Watson, but let me continue. On the night of Mary's death, he had been with her earlier in the evening, at which time she was in the company of another woman, almost certainly a fellow unfortunate. Indeed, Mary was known to share her accommodation with other such women out of pity for them, something that would have infuriated Barnett. Although he was separated from Mary at the time, having argued with her recently, it is likely that he still retained a key to her lodgings so would have had opportunity."

"Was he interviewed by the police?"

"Oh, yes. He was questioned just four hours after her death and his clothes examined for blood stains. Detective Inspector Abberline, a good man, was satisfied with his alibi of being at his lodging house all evening since he had left Mary, but it would have been possible for him to slip out unnoticed if he had wanted."

"I suppose that as a boyfriend of a prostitute he would have been known and trusted by the other victims, which would be an advantage if he were the Ripper."

"Quite so. There was also a possible coincidence, and you know how much I hate coincidences, Watson, in that following Annie Chapman's murder ... she was the second victim ... a torn piece of an envelope was discovered close to the body, it being speculated that she had been holding it at the time of her demise. That fragment revealed part of an address which some claim was that of Barnett, who at that time would have still been living with Mary Kelly. Whether it was a letter written to

Barnett, or the return address to him, or something completely unrelated is not clear ... the handwriting was never subjected to analysis, and by the time I got to hear about this document it had gone missing, which in itself is suspicious. Hence as I was never able to examine it first hand, I must discount the theories surrounding it as being unreliable at best.[4]"

"And your conclusion about Barnett, Holmes?"

"I cannot entirely rule him out, Watson. Although, having read Abberline's report I am inclined to defer to his judgement. Also, I cannot see the suggested motive as being sound either, and so on balance I discount him from being the Ripper."

That completes the list, Holmes. What next ... Whitechapel?"

"No, my friend, we are far too early. I am not as young and energetic as I used to be and it has been a long and tiring day already, so with Mrs. Hudson's permission I will avail myself of the comforts of her sofa and rest, while you return to your lodgings and your wife. However, be sure to be back here by ten-thirty as we have a long night ahead of us. Don't forget to leave the Ripper File as I wouldn't want you to get ahead of yourself."

I found Mrs. Hudson in her kitchen, and explained the situation to her. Under the circumstances, she was more than happy for Holmes to remain, almost to the extent of being apologetic.

"He could have had his old room, but I've recently rented it out to a kindly old man. I don't know why he wants it really given all his injuries from some mountaineering accident abroad he says. I mean he can hardly get up them stairs in his condition, but he insists that the accommodation is ideal for his purpose as he just wants somewhere quiet where he can write. Retired now, but worked as a professor at the university. He told me that he studied the mathematics of moving objects or some such thing ... no future in that I told him."

---

[4] According to a posting on casebook.org by Dr. Frederick Walker the fragment in question contained a capital letter 'M', the letters 'Sp' and the number '2' which he was claimed were part of Mary Kelly's address at Miller's Court, Spitalfields, 26 Dorset Street. This hypothesis has largely been rebuffed by other Ripperologists.

"Quite so," said I hearing, but not really listening to what she was saying, as I made for the front door and home.

Chapter Four

Whitechapel

Upon my return to Baker Street and seeing Holmes lying there on the sofa fast asleep I just could not resist using the instruction that he had spoken to me so often in the past.

"Come, Holmes, come. The game is afoot!"

"Very droll, Watson. What time is it?"

"It has just gone half past ten and I have a cab waiting outside."

"Well, you may dismiss it as we will be travelling by Underground tonight."

"Oh, God, you know I abhor that form of transport ever since you forced me to use it in the case of the *Red-Headed League*. Smoky, dirty, and overcrowded ... there had better be a good reason, Holmes."

"I assure you that there is, and it has the added advantage of being much cheaper than a cab. Now then are you going to produce your envelope before we leave?"

"Envelope, what envelope?"

"You know as well as I that when you came down to visit me in Sussex that it was with the sole purpose of a challenge with respect to our fiend Jack the Ripper. Do you not think that I am fully aware that you, too, followed those murders with interest at the time, and no doubt came to your own conclusions?"

He paused while he took an envelope out from the inner pocket of his frock coat. He held it aloft before placing it on the table.

"Here is my solution, but where is yours?"

"I am glad to see that your powers of deduction have not faded in the past five years. You are, of course, correct and in order to be absolutely fair in this challenge as you call it, I have made my initial conclusions in this document."

At this juncture I also produced an envelope from my coat pocket and placed it on top of Holmes's.

"However, I reserve the right to make amendments should our investigation tonight warrant it."

"That sounds fair enough. Let us take these unopened documents with us, and return to them over lunch tomorrow for I fear that we will both be in no fit state for breakfast after this evening's sojourn."

"Would you be prepared to make a wager, Holmes?"

"I don't see how we can do that for there would be no way of proving whether either of us is correct in our deductions given that after all this time it is unlikely that the true identity of Jack the Ripper will ever be forthcoming."

"No, you misunderstand. I mean as to whether I will come up with the same solution as you did, thus making my powers of deduction equal to your own."

"Hmm, that is an interesting proposition. Are you sure that you can afford to lose even more money on top of your usual gambling debts?"

"You don't seem to have much confidence in me ... I was hoping that my winnings would cancel those particular debts in full. The real question is, how confident are you in your own conclusions?"

Holmes stared at me for some moments before making a decision.

"Fine, I don't want to take money from you, old friend, but if our solutions are in accord, I will pay off your creditors, but if not you will take me to Wigmore Hall tomorrow afternoon, followed by dinner at Simpson's, and promise that for the next year that you will periodically dispatch to Sussex quantities of my favourite shag from Bradley's in Oxford Street."

"Agreed," said I without hesitation and shaking his hand to seal the bargain.

"Now we must be away as time is short. You take charge of the Ripper File," said he, handing me the volume in question.

In minutes we were standing on the Metropolitan Railway platform at Baker Street station awaiting our train. My apprehension regarding travel by the Underground system proved unfounded as the station was cavernous and bright with few passengers at that time of the evening. Most gratifying of all was that there was no sign of that choking smoke from the very many steam locomotives that must pass through the station every day, smoke which had branded the Underground as no place for a gentleman to be seen. Holmes noted my surprise.

"Not as fearful as you suspected, Watson. I really do think that you should keep up with the times for even I down in Sussex had read of the introduction of electric locomotives on this line some two years ago."

Soon enough our train arrived and in under thirty minutes we were at our destination, having traversed what I always regarded as being the northern boundary of London, passing Portland Road, Gower Street for Euston station, and King's Cross (which I noted the Metropolitan Railway had decided to spell without an apostrophe). From here the railway veered to the right and toward the city itself with the next station being Farringdon, then past the sidings which served Smithfield market to Aldersgate, and on to Moorgate and Bishopsgate (which also served as the stop for the much larger railway terminus of Liverpool Street). The tracks now divided with the right-hand branch going to Aldgate and on to Mark Lane and along the river heading westward, while our train continued eastward to Aldgate East where it joined the District Railway, and finally up a steep incline to St. Mary's, the church after which the area of Whitechapel is named (this time with an apostrophe), and finally to Whitechapel itself. I was eager to exit the station and start our investigation, but Holmes held out an arm to stop me.

"I trust that you will remember the route we took this night, for it will prove instructive later. Now tell me, Watson, what do you note about this station?"

I looked around and surveyed the scene.

"It is much larger than I expected with wide platforms and sidings, and I am surprised that it is open to the elements for an Underground station."

"Very good, Watson. You see at the time of Jack the Ripper this was the terminus for the District Railway, and hence needed the extra capacity. Then its name was Whitechapel Mile End. The line was only extended further eastward to Bow in 1902. Of course, until recently it was served by steam locomotives, the Beyer Peacock condensing type to be precise. These had the advantage of being able to recover the exhaust steam that you rightly found so obnoxious via the water tanks, but when not working the steam would be directed to the blast pipe and up the chimney in the usual way. Hence having an open terminus was an advantage to let off all that steam. But come this way as there is something I wish to show you."

He walked along the platform, almost to where it ended at the Bow end of the station, and pointed up at a building on the north side.

"Do you see that beacon of hope to the future, Watson?"

"The board school you mean," said I, recognising the standard red brickwork design of such establishments.

"Indeed. It is the former Buck's Row Board School [12] which opened in 1877, but more importantly it is just along from there that our first victim met their end. Now you see that retaining wall [13] which runs along from the vicinity of the school parallel to the tracks ..."

"Yes."

"Well, do you think that you could climb over it from the school side and get down to the platform without injury?"

"If I were a few years younger I dare say that I would have no trouble climbing on top of that wall, but then it must be all of a thirty-foot drop down to the tracks ... I note the ledge about half way down, so if I could lower myself to it first and then make a jump, I think I would stand a fair chance. That ledge though is only a single brick wide, and in the dark I would be fortunate indeed to make it unharmed, so on balance I estimate that I could do it and survive, but I would be very likely to get a broken leg or worse for my efforts."

"And what if I asked you to do it when there was a train being stabled overnight on the line adjacent to the wall?"

His question brought back memories of the *Adventure of the Bruce-Partington Plans* and the body of the unfortunate Cadogan West falling from the roof of a moving Underground train as it passed over the points at Aldgate, not so far away from where I now stood contemplating something similar.

"You mean could Jack the Ripper escape the scene by climbing over that wall and dropping down on to a carriage roof, probably no more than a fifteen-foot drop, and from there down to the platform?"

"I do."

"Yes, that would be quite possible in my opinion. Is that how you think he made his escape undetected?"

"Not necessarily, but keep it in mind as we walk, Watson."

Just then there was a rumble which startled me.

"Don't worry, it is just a train coming into one of the platforms beneath us. You see, the first service to Whitechapel was by the tracks of East London Railway from Liverpool Street to Wapping and then through Brunel's tunnel to south London. Did you not notice the curve branching off the main line shortly after we left St. Mary's which connects the two lines?"

I did not respond as I had had my fill of Underground railway history for one night. As we exited the station Holmes pointed out another beacon to the future. This time it wasn't a board school, but the Working Lads Institute [14] adjacent to the station entrance.

"As you can see from the stonework it was built in 1885 and has been keeping young lads out of trouble ever since. It provides academic classes, and has a gymnasium, a library, a swimming pool, and even limited accommodation."

37

"Better facilities, Holmes, than some gentlemen's clubs in the West End that I have known."

"It might also interest you to learn that the inquest of our first two victims was held there." He paused for a moment before continuing. "Now look around you, Watson, and give me your opinion of the area at this time of night."

"Whitechapel Road is a wide and busy thoroughfare even at this hour. It is after all one of the main arteries out of London to Essex and beyond. It also shouldn't surprise you that I know this street quite well," said I, pointing to the façade of the London Hospital [15] on the opposite side of the road.

"Forgive me, Watson, of course, you must have visited here on many an occasion in a professional capacity. There was I concentrating on the Lads Institute to illustrate that the area is not all sadness and full of tragic events when I overlooked the most obvious example to prove my point."

"Just a few doors along from here is another example, Holmes." I indicated a non-descript shop front with my walking cane. "Do you remember that poor man Joseph Merrick? He was put on display in the back room of that building, like some circus freak, prior to Dr. Frederick Treves accommodating him at the hospital. It was only due to public sympathy and subsequent donations that he was able to remain in residence, living without fear for the rest of his largely unhappy life?"

"That must have been around four years before the Ripper murders … I recall well enough accounts of people viewing the person that they called the Elephant Man."

"The whole of the East End is changing for the better, Holmes. Many of the old squalid houses and ways have been swept away and replaced with model dwellings for the working classes."

"But in 1888 there was still much poverty here. Whitechapel Road may have looked respectable enough, but the same was not true of where Polly Nichols met her end. I believe that your memory fails you as to what you remember it was like twenty years ago, both here and in the West End."

"I am bound to say that I disagree with you, Holmes. In 1888 London was surely at the centre of the greatest empire ever known, an empire based on trade, justice, the English language, and culture. Queen Victoria had been on the throne for over half a century and there was stability. The British ruled a quarter of the world, and English was spoken by around forty percent of the world's population of one-and-a-half billion people. Those dominions, colonies, and protectorates where ultimately administered from London, and it was true to say that what Britain did not already have in its grasp it did not want."

"I suspect then that you would agree with Dr. Samuel Johnson when he put it to James Boswell that 'Why, Sir, you find no man, at all intellectual, who is willing to leave London. No, Sir, when a man is tired of London, he is tired of life; for there is in London all that life can afford'."

"Indeed, I do, Holmes. London is the largest jewel in the imperial crown, and the West End the centre for opulence, light, the arts, and the latest scientific inventions."

"That is on the surface only, Watson. Beneath that golden veneer of respectability is a different reality for millions. As you rightly say the empire was built ostensibly on trade, and therefore the great ports and manufacturing cities of Birmingham, Manchester, Bristol, Liverpool and the like all played their part. London was like the world's central exchange, a cosmopolitan city unlike any other attracting the poor and those looking for a new start in life. The vast majority of those people never made it to the West End where we were fortunate enough to reside, but by necessity accumulated close to the docks, where the poor worked and lived among the influx of people from overseas who arrived on ships from which they could not afford to travel far. This part of London, the East End, only offered poverty, squalor, darkness, overcrowding, homelessness, and starvation [16]. How many people do you think lived in Whitechapel at the time of the Ripper?"

"I don't really know, maybe fifty thousand," I replied taking an educated guess based upon the size of the area compared with a similar one in the West End which I knew well.

"Not even close, Watson. Some nine-hundred thousand lived in the East End with a quarter of those being in Whitechapel. Most lived in common lodging houses [17], and the overcrowded slums made up of courts and alleyways [18] where more than one family might occupy a single room … many just lived on the streets, and most sought solace in the public houses. Even if you were lucky enough to be a resident at one of the many common lodging houses you still had to be out and on the streets during the day. Your chances of living to a ripe old age were slim. As a doctor you might recall that infant mortality was around one in four."

"But there was surely no need for such poverty, the country was booming … there must have been work for all those who wanted it, Holmes."

"Oh, how your memory fails you, Watson. 1888 was in the middle of what was termed The Long Depression. Work was intermittent with the largest employer, the docks [19], taking people on a day-by-day basis as was required. There were, naturally, other employers but all paid low wages … maybe £1 or £2 per week, and falling from year-to-year due to the recession. If you were lucky enough to find employment you would be expected to work for up to twenty hours a day, with children and women being expected to work when they could. No wonder then that so many women became part-time prostitutes, with most unfortunates also becoming chronic alcoholics."

"Yes, I do remember the advertising slogan of the time, 'drunk for a penny, dead drunk for tuppence'."

"Quite so, Watson. Most do not realise that the East End was really an amalgamation of different peoples all living side-by-side relatively peacefully. At Aldgate were the Germans who specialised in sugar manufacture, at Spitalfields there were what was left of the Huguenots who had been known for their silks and later furniture making, while Limehouse was dominated by the Indian and Chinese communities of sailors.

There was also the influx of fifty thousand Jews from Russia, Poland, and Germany [20] who ensured that they were represented in every community, and dominant in some. With work at a premium, it is not surprising that various groups of people became vilified for stealing English jobs and adding to the problems that already existed ... what is most surprising to me is that there were not more serious crimes committed in the East End, for whereas thieving was rife, the number of murders as a percentage of the population was actually less than elsewhere in the Metropolis."

I decided to change tact, and return to the reason why we were here in Whitechapel in the first place.

"Thinking about our victims, Holmes, what could an unfortunate expect from a client other than contracting a disease and the threat of violence."

"If you were young and attractive perhaps half-a-crown, or if very lucky ten shillings, but the women who became the victims of the Ripper would have been due to receive only a fraction of that amount ... for which they lost their lives in the most gruesome of ways."

We both reflected upon that statement for a long moment before Holmes broke the silence.

Come, Watson, we have much to do."

Chapter Five

Mary Ann 'Polly' Nichols

We proceeded east along the Whitechapel Road taking the first left turning into Brady Street, and then not the next left, Winthrop Street, but the second into Durward Street so that we now had the board school directly in front of us on the left-hand side of that narrow road. In just those few paces the whole atmosphere of the area had changed from one of relative bustle to a dreary silence and darkness despite the street lights doing their best to bring cheer to the scene. On the corner was the Roebuck public house and extending down the right-hand side of the thoroughfare was a wool warehouse. The road was clearly divided into commercial properties to the right, and a long line of terrace houses to the left [21] such that each property had a door directly on to the street and a single downstairs window with two above. The workmanship was superior to some areas I had witnessed with there being a step up to the pairs of front doors, which had a brick arch over them. The terrace ended abruptly after around twenty properties as it was broken by what appeared from this distance to be a large gate to a builders' yard or some such establishment. Beyond that the road spanned the East London Line, and then the board school, which loomed a little like a master towering over his pupils all seated at their desks. Holmes walked up to the wooden gate [22] and proclaimed, "This is Brown's stable-yard, and it was here in front of these gates that Polly Nichols met her demise, Watson. What information does the Ripper File reveal about the circumstances?"

43

Hurriedly I found the relevant pages and made a summary of the content.

"The body was found by Police Constable John Neil [23] at 3.45 a.m. on the thirty-first of August ..."

"And what day of the week was that, Watson?"

"It was a Friday morning, Holmes. Is that significant?"

"That is for you to ponder, my friend. But I will add that it was the Friday morning of a Bank Holiday weekend."

I thought no more upon that fact, and continued my narrative.

"It was lying on the pavement by the stable-yard opposite Essex Wharf in Buck's Row ... but we are in Durward Street, Holmes ..."

"I know, the name of the street was changed in 1892."

"It says that at first Neil assumed that the woman had simply fallen down drunk, and was sleeping off the effects of the alcohol ... something I expect that was all too frequent around here. However, on closer examination he saw that her face was bloodied and that her throat had been cut across from ear-to-ear."

"But Neil was not the first to come across Mary Nichols that morning, if I remember correctly?"

"Indeed, just a few minutes earlier at around 3.40 a.m. two horse-cart drivers named Charles Cross and Robert Paul passed the same spot on their way to work. They had both noticed the woman on her back, with her skirt raised almost to her abdomen, and they too assumed that she was dead drunk. However, they did have the decency to pull her skirt back down, and then went on their way, vowing to inform the first policeman that they came across."

"That would have been Police Constable Jonas Mizen who they found close to the junction of Hanbury Street with Baker's Row," said Holmes, pointing in the direction of the said location to the west of our current position.

"Police Constable Neil was soon joined by Police Constable John Thain who confirmed that when he passed Essex Wharf at 3.30 a.m. the body was not there."

"Now tell me what does the Ripper File say about her prior movements?"

"These seem to be well documented. At 11.00 p.m. she was seen walking along the Whitechapel Road, then at 12.30 a.m. she was spotted leaving the Frying Pan public house on the corner of Brick Lane and Thrawl Street. From here she returned to her lodging house at No. 18 Thawl Street, but was thrown out as she didn't have the 4d. fee for the night. Her last known appearance was around 2.30 a.m. in Osborn Street where it meets Whitechapel Road [24]. This was verified by Emily Holland, a fellow unfortunate and sometime room-mate, with whom she spoke for around eight minutes. Holland revealed that Nichols was very drunk and was off to try and obtain money for her lodgings, something Nichols thought she would have no trouble doing given that she was wearing a new bonnet."

"So can you construct how she came to be here, Watson?"

"Well, she was undoubtedly looking for clients that evening, and visited at least one public house where she had become intoxicated. It seems obvious to me that the drink was paid for with her doss house funds, and hence she was ejected from her lodging and went back on the streets in the hope of finding another client. At that time of morning only the main thoroughfares such as Whitechapel Road would still be busy, and so it was that having left Emily Holland she walked in search of a prospect. She was lucky, or rather most unlucky, in that the client she picked up was Jack the Ripper, and that must have happened somewhere in the vicinity of the London Hospital, which at all times of day and night has people coming and going. The problem was that she now needed somewhere a little more private to entertain her client, and hence she led him around to Buck's Row, probably in the knowledge of the stable yard that would afford some privacy. In her trade I suspect she would have a good knowledge of such locations in an area given that she had no room of her own to which she could take a man. Maybe from experience she knew that the gate was usually left open or unlocked. It is of no consequence for Nichols decided upon bringing her client here, and then paid the price for it with her life sometime after 3.30 a.m., but before 3.40 a.m."

"Excellent, Watson. I concur that is exactly what happened that morning. Later that day the police did make enquiries at the various public houses in the area, The Grave Maurice and The King's Arms, as well as The Roebuck, but nobody seems to have noted the presence of Nichols so we are safe to assume that she picked up her client along the main road. This can also be inferred since at that time of morning the establishments would most likely be closed, and moreover from the fact that upon examining her possessions no money was found."

"She never did get her 4d. for her lodgings then ... poor woman," I commented sadly.

"I made further enquiries at the time to ascertain whether the stable-yard gate was open or closed, but alas nobody seems to have noticed, or thought to check. What happened next, Watson?"

I returned to the Ripper File **[25]**.

"It seems that Police Constable Thain went to fetch a local doctor, Rees Ralph Llewellyn, while Police Constable Mizen, who was now also at the scene, went to collect an ambulance to convey the body to the nearest mortuary. Meanwhile Police Constable Neil made enquiries at properties in the immediate area. These came to nothing as it seems that nobody saw anything, and only one person, a Mrs. Green who lived at No. 6 right next to the stable-yard, heard what she took to be an argument between a man and a woman ... something not unusual in the least."

I paused as I had come to the section that listed the injuries received by poor Polly Nichols. Even though I am a medical man who has seen death countless times on the fields of battle, it did not prepare me fully for what I now read aloud to Holmes.

"According to Dr. Llewellyn in addition to her head being almost severed **[26]**, the abdomen had been ripped up, and the bowels were protruding. The abdominal wall, the whole length of the body, had been cut open, and on either side were two incised wounds almost as severe as the centre one. They

46

reached from the lower part of the abdomen to the breast-bone."

"You will need a stronger stomach than this if you are to survive the night," said Holmes, seeing my obvious discomfort. "The injuries inflicted upon Nichols were not as severe as those to later victims, which has led many to conclude that the killer was interrupted."

"By the approach of Cross and Paul, no doubt," I added.

"Indeed, but that does beg another question does it not?"

I examined a map of the area that Holmes had made as part of his notes [27].

"I see what you are implying … Buck's Row had few options for escape. Police Constable Neil was approaching from the east, and the horse-cart men and Police Constable Mizen were doing the same from the west, so how did the murderer manage to evade being seen? There were just ten minutes between the street being empty at 3.30 a.m. when Police Constable Thain came past, and the body of Nichols being found by the horse-cart men at 3.40 a.m. … it must have taken several minutes to inflict the wounds, so surely whichever direction the Ripper took along Buck's Row after that he would have been spotted by someone?"

Only now did I understood fully why Holmes had questioned me on the platform at Whitechapel station.

"Of course, Holmes, the Ripper did have another option. First, if the gate was open, or the yard accessible, he could enter and climb over the back wall undetected into Winthrop Street, on the opposite side of which is the retaining wall to the Underground station … and as already discussed it might be possible to scale that wall and drop down on to the platform unharmed … in fact, in his heightened state he would surely have been able to do so."

"Alternatively?"

"Alternatively, if he continued along Buck's Row as far as the board school, he could have accessed Winthrop Street from its junction with Buck's Row, and if he didn't fancy scaling the wall to the station, he could have doubled back to Brady Street."

"A third possibility also presents itself in that Spitalfields Coal Depot backs on to Buck's Row where the street widens past the board school. Another wall to scale, but the coal yard could have been easily accessed. And what did the police conclude, Watson?"

"There is nothing here about that, Holmes."

"Exactly, and so what do you deduce?"

I hesitated as I could see nothing of import from the lack of information.

"Come, Watson, they could not say which escape route the Ripper took because something was missing."

"Is this another case of the dog in the night time, Holmes?"

Holmes smiled as he recognised my allusion to the mystery I entitled *The Adventure of Silver Blaze.*

"Blood, Watson, blood was missing. You cannot attack somebody like that without getting covered in it yourself. You have probably never heard, or read, about the slaughter of the Marr family at their draper's shop along the Ratcliff Highway in Wapping."

"I cannot say that I have."

"It was on a December night in 1811 that an unknown assailant gained entry to their shop, where they also lived, and brutally murdered Timothy Marr, the husband, his wife Celia, his fourteen-week-old son, also called Timothy, and an apprentice named James Gowan. This, of course, was at the time of the Bow Street Runners, nearly two decades before the formation of the Metropolitan Police, so there was little official help to be had. However, such was the amount of blood that the good citizens of Wapping were able to follow the trail for over half a mile. I daresay that there was nowhere near the same volume of liquid in this case, but I would have expected some blood to adhere to the Ripper's clothing, particularly to coat the uppers and soles of his shoes, from which traces would be found on the pavement, so indicating which way he went."

"It was still dark don't forget, Holmes. Maybe the police looked, but couldn't find anything."

"That may be the answer, but more likely that they never looked in the first place. Incredibly it was even suggested that

48

no crime had been perpetrated, and that Nichols had committed suicide by cutting her own throat."

"Impossible!" said I, without any hesitation.

"Ask yourself this, Watson ... even if not here, surely there would be some blood trails to follow at one of the other murder sites, especially since those deaths were far more gruesome?

"Perhaps not, Holmes. Would the blood not soak into the Ripper's clothing, rather than drip all over the place?"

"An excellent question, and one to which I have given considerable thought, though I must admit that my researches in this field of science are far from complete. However, I can tell you with some confidence that transfer blood stains tend to impregnate the weave of a fabric, whereas splatter droplets remain on the surface of the material due to the angle of contact and the surface tension, which naturally varies from fabric to fabric. In the case of the Ripper, you would expect the majority of blood to be splatter droplets, which would build up on the surface of the cloth until viscosity and gravity predominate. Hence after just a minute following such an event, I would expect to see signs of blood droplets on the pavement that had originated from the clothes of the perpetrator, and that this would continue for up to thirty minutes, which I estimate to be the drying time of blood outdoors on a cold night."

"There is another possible explanation for the lack of blood," said I.

"If there is something I have overlooked I would be glad to learn of it."

"Supposing that the Ripper did not work alone, and used a coach to pick up the unfortunates, murdered them inside the carriage, and then just dumped them at the roadside ... then there would be very little blood." I genuinely thought that I had come up with a solid solution, which Holmes had not considered. Holmes though just sighed.

"Shall I show you why that theory does not even get past the starting gate?"

Reluctantly I nodded in the full knowledge that my theory was about to be struck down. Holmes crossed the road to Essex Wharf where he approached a dustbin that had been placed by the kerb. He took off the lid, which he placed on the pavement, and having ascertained that the bin was empty tipped it on its side and positioned it on the road itself. He then gave it a gentle push causing it to roll slowly down the street. As it did so the noise of metal upon tarmac, emulating that of carriage wheel upon road, brought several of the residents of Durward Street to their windows to peer out upon the strange spectacle.

"You see my point, Watson?"

"Yes, the noise of a carriage passing at that time of night, and in this area, would be so unusual that it would immediately attract interest."

"It certainly would given that none of these good people could ever afford to keep their own vehicle, and that nobody would ever take a carriage to visit anybody along this road, it would stick out like a sore thumb."

"Now what does your file tell us of Nichols herself?"

"She was five-feet-two-inches tall, had a small scar on her forehead, three missing teeth, though some reports claim that it was five, brown hair that was turning grey, a dark complexion, and was forty-three-years old. Her only possessions were a comb, along with a broken fragment of a mirror, and a white handkerchief. She was wearing a reddish-brown Ulster coat, a newish brown linsey frock, two petticoats, a pair of men's boots, and a new black straw bonnet trimmed with black velvet. It later transpired that she was estranged from William Nichols, whom she had married in 1864 and by whom she had had five children."

"The poor woman. Not much to show for forty-three years of life is it, Watson?" commented Holmes, in a somewhat philosophical tone. "Finally, can you tell me what the police investigation concluded?"

"Dr. Llewellyn stated that, 'she was ripped open just as you see a dead calf at the butcher's'. At first, he thought that her killer had been left-handed, but he later retracted this statement. By all accounts the police did their job diligently in that they searched over two hundred common lodging houses, and actually made fourteen arrests, none of which came to anything. It was thought that she had probably been attacked by a gang, a seaman, or somebody who worked as a slaughterman or butcher … in the main because of Dr. Llewellyn's comments."

"There was little more that they could do especially since being the first in the series the police at that time did not know that there was worse to follow … and follow it did, just two days after Nichols was buried at the City of London Cemetery at Manor Park."

"I suppose it was just seen as another violent death of an East End unfortunate," said I, still reflecting on what a waste of a life it was under any circumstance.

"Are you ready to visit the next crime scene, Watson?"

"Yes, lead on, Holmes."

Chapter Six

Annie Chapman

Holmes led as we walked along Durward Street and after a couple more turns we found ourselves in Hanbury Street. Along the way we passed another of those beacons to the future in the shape of Deal Street school, an establishment built in 1895 under the auspices of the London School Board. It was unusual in that because of the shortage of space for the thousand plus pupils the playground was constructed on the roof. Holmes also pointed out The Alma public house on the corner of Spelman Street, but informed me that it was at another such premises, The Ten Bells in Commercial Road, where the second victim, Annie Chapman, had been seen leaving in the company of a man, possibly Jack the Ripper, on the night of her murder. Eventually we crossed the main thoroughfare of Brick Lane and stopped a few doors further down outside No. 29 Hanbury Street [28] on the right-hand side.

"No comment to make, Watson?"

"Only that we seem to have walked some considerable distance [29]."

"Indeed, we have, old friend. We passed over the parish boundary of St. Mary Whitechapel some time ago and are now in the heart of Christ Church, Spitalfields, and what remains of Huguenot London. Interesting don't you think that despite being called the Whitechapel murders, only one of the five that we are investigating tonight actually took place in that parish?"

"Strictly speaking that may be correct, Holmes, but most people would not know of the parish boundaries and would still refer to the whole area as Whitechapel," I retorted.

Holmes paused and then pointed to a substantial brick building with both large and small arched windows [30] on the opposite side of the road.

"That is Hanbury Hall," said he. "It was built in the early 18th century as a small French Protestant chapel, but is now part of the Anglican Christ Church which so dominates this area."

"I do believe that I have visited Hanbury Hall in the past, Holmes. If I am not mistaken, I came here to listen to Charles Dickens who was giving a public reading of one of his many works."

"In this instance your memory is quite sound for he was a regular visitor to the building, but in 1888 it was also where the so called 'match girls' held their strike meetings as they began their protest for better working conditions at the Bryant and May factory in Bow."

Instinctively I opened Holmes's file, and having found the relevant pages began reading out aloud the entry for Jack the Ripper's second victim.

"Annie Chapman, also known as Annie Siffey, Annie Sivvy, and 'Dark Annie', was murdered on the eighth of September 1888 with her body being found at the rear of No. 29 Hanbury Street."

"That was a Saturday," added Holmes.

"Annie was forty-seven years old, five-feet tall, with dark brown hair, and a large thick nose. She was wearing a black figured jacket, brown bodice, black skirt, and lace boots. Generally, she was in poor health, and had been given medication for what was thought to be lung disease from which she was expected to succumb in just a few months. She had been married to John Chapman, a coachman, by whom she had had eight children, but he had died in 1886 since when she had been living at a common lodging house at No. 30 Dorset Street with a sieve-maker for whom she also worked."

"And what about her movements on the night in question?"

"Again, these seem well documented, Holmes. At 2 a.m. she had spoken with Timothy Donovan, the deputy at a lodging house at No. 35 Dorset Street, where she had hoped to gain entry even though, just like Polly Nichols, she did not have the doss money for the night."

"She probably knew that she stood no chance of going to her normal lodging, so thought that she would try her luck down the road as it were," conjectured Holmes.

"It did her no good and she was asked to leave, though she said that she would return later once she had the necessary money. It was also noted by Donovan that she was drunk. At around 4.45 a.m., John Richardson a resident at No.29 entered the back yard to check if the cellar was padlocked, and also to trim a loose piece of leather from his boot ... he sat on the back step to do this, and noticed nothing untoward."

"A rather strange time don't you think for such activities, Watson?"

"Indeed, but surely if he were the Ripper, he would either not have come forward to volunteer any information, or at the very least come up with a more believable reason for being there at that time of day."

"A very good point, Watson. Do continue."

"Next at 5.15 a.m., Albert Cadosch, a neighbour at No. 27 went into his yard to use the lavatory. He says that he heard a woman saying 'No' before the sound of what he interpreted as somebody falling against the fence that separated the two properties. He did not investigate further, but at about the same time a Mrs. Elizabeth Long said that she saw a woman in the company of a man close to The Ten Bells public house. She gave a description of the fellow as being foreign, with dark hair, and wearing a deerstalker hat and a dark overcoat. He had a shabby genteel appearance ..."

"Before you say anything further, Watson, I assure you that it was not I. You know full well that I only wear such a hat in the country as it would be out of place in a city setting. That Sidney Paget has a lot to answer for in making that piece of apparel so popular and an acceptable form of headwear about town."

"What is known though, is that at 6.00 a.m. John Davis, another resident at No. 29, ventured into the yard and found Annie Chapman's body close to the back steps and partition fence [31] ... do you want me to read the newspaper clipping of her injuries that you have pasted into your file from the *East London Observer*?"

"Yes, they will be instructive in that it will indicate just how gruesome they were, and what the Ripper was capable of in such a short time. However, I should point out that it was written by a journalist at the time with a degree of hyperbole added for the gratification of the reader, and also differs dramatically from the facts presented in the subsequent official police report."

I took a deep breath and began to read the catalogue of horrific wounds that had been inflicted on the already far from healthy Annie Chapman.

"A woman [32] lay there with her clothes so disarranged as to expose her knees drawn up as if in agony, together with the lower portion of the abdomen, which had been mutilated in a frightful manner, the intestines, with the viscera and the heart, having been literally torn out of the mangled body and laid by her side. The head of the woman was turned back, revealing an enormous gash, so broad and so deep as almost to have severed the connection with the body. The face ... that of a woman of about forty ... was deadly white, and the hair, which was wavy brown, was slightly disarranged. Portions of the flesh on the lower part of the body hung in shreds, the dress was bespattered with blood ... as, indeed, was a portion of the fencing, as if it had received a spurt from a severed artery ... beside the woman two pools of blood had formed, and upon her shoulders were slashes of blood and some of the viscera. Her head was lying towards the house, and her feet towards the end of the yard ... this is just as you warned me, Holmes, much worse than the first murder."

"Note, Watson, the specific mention of pools of blood, and that blood had been splattered onto the fence."

"Your earlier argument is well noted ... Jack the Ripper could not have escaped without getting covered in blood himself, which begs the question as to why no trail was found that could be followed."

"And there is more, Watson, for what was not mentioned in the newspaper report was that a section of the stomach wall, most of the bladder and part of the reproductive organs were all missing. She had also been partially strangulated ... no doubt to make her unconscious while her dissection was performed. In addition, her wedding and keeper rings were missing, having been pulled from her fingers."

Over the page were the conclusions of George Bagster Phillips the divisional surgeon of police. I read the findings aloud.

"It seemed clear that both victims were killed by the same person who possessed some anatomical knowledge, and who wanted to keep some body parts as a trophy. It was also thought that the murder weapon was a small blade about six to eight inches in length, either an amputating knife or possibly an implement such as might be used by a slaughterman. This, of course, did not change the verdict of wilful murder by person or persons unknown ... a verdict reached at the Working Lads Institute after an inquest lasting five days."

"If you read on you will see that the police acted quickly and quite correctly [33]. As you are aware I am often critical of the lack of imagination shown by their detectives, but for general investigative duties where large numbers of men are needed there is no finer body that I would rather trust."

I did as I was instructed.

"On the day of the murder the police acted swiftly. Several officers were placed on plain-clothes duty, interviews were conducted with all the inhabitants of No. 29 as well as at the adjoining houses. Common lodging houses in the area were visited to see if anybody had arrived there with blood about their person, pawnbrokers and jewellers were also visited to see if Chapman's missing rings could be traced, public houses inspected to get more information about her last movements and any of her clients that night, and information circulated about possible suspects. Soon the whole police investigation was placed under the sole control of Chief Inspector Donald

Swanson **[34]** by order of Sir Charles Warren **[35]**, the Metropolitan Police Commissioner."

"Both good men, Watson, but it didn't stop there by any means. The police advised that the women should walk in pairs, and carry whistles. Many were to secretly arm themselves. Soon an extra twenty-seven plain-clothes officers were placed on the beat and as from the October other uniformed officers were drafted in. In addition, there were some rather strange suggestions in that Scotland Yard were asked to consider disguising men as women prostitutes, have boxers dressed as women and wearing steel collars for protection, and that the eyes of the victims should be photographed in the belief that the retina captured and retained the last image the victims saw."

"And despite all this the police got nowhere. In fact, it says here that in a letter to the Home Office, Charles Warren complained that the reporters of the press were hampering the investigations by following the detectives everywhere they went. And in retaliation the press turned on the police, hinting of their incompetence."

"It was also now that the red herrings started to appear, Watson. The first was that fragment of the envelope we have already discussed in relation to Joseph Barnett. Then there was a leather apron found in the backyard at No. 29. It actually belonged to John Richardson, but at the time it fuelled speculation in the press, first mentioned in connection with the murder of Nichols, that the culprit was someone who used a leather apron for work, and was most likely of Jewish origin. The hunt for 'Leather Apron' **[36]** was afoot with posters to that effect being placed all over the East End."

"Yes, it says here that one poor individual named John Piser, though in some documents he is called Pizer, a 38-year-old Polish Jew who made boots from leather, and was known locally as 'Leather Apron' was arrested on the tenth of September for no other reason than that he had 'a cruel and sardonic look', used knives in his work, and used to be taunted by children ... it was enough to make him an immediate suspect despite his having alibis for the nights in question. The accusation was so libellous that he was later able to get compensation from the newspaper that had named him as the prime suspect in the Whitechapel murders."

"He was by no means the only one, Watson ... suspects were quite plentiful and all had to be eliminated. There was William Piggott a ship's cook, Edward McKenna an itinerant pedlar, Jacob Isenschmidt a mentally ill man who had been a pork butcher, Oswald Puckeridge another mentally ill man who had surgical training and who had recently been released from an asylum, and an unknown American physician who in 1887, and probably later in 1888, had offered £20 per fresh body organ ... not one that had been preserved in alcohol, but a body part direct from the newly deceased."

"How bizarre ... and you investigated each of these leads?"

"No, no, Watson. The official forces were quite capable of easily eliminating all these fellows. In the case of the American doctor, I doubt if he even existed, and was probably just a prank by some medical students."

"I too have sympathy for the police, since there was no firm evidence upon which they could act."

"They were very soon, though, to have a name for the fiend ... and that was the biggest red herring of all," stated Holmes.

"Ah, yes, that came via the Central News Agency in the form of a letter that commenced 'Dear Boss' [37], and was signed 'Jack the Ripper'."

"The only genuine aspect about it was when it said 'that joke about Leather Apron gave me the fits'. I believe that the letter was a fake sent by a reporter hoping to increase the circulation of his newspaper."

I looked all around me so as to be sure of our location, and that what I would say next would not be immediately shot down by Holmes.

"I have been thinking ..."

"A good start," interrupted Holmes, with more than a hint of sarcasm in his voice. A positive sign I thought as it meant that he was actually beginning to enjoy our investigation together.

"For Polly Nichols, you convinced me that the most likely escape route was via either the adjacent Underground station, or the nearby goods yard. Here though the closest station must be Liverpool Street, a good quarter of a mile away in which case I put it to you that the Ripper would have been seen by at least one witness?"

"So how do you think the fiend managed to escape detection this time, Watson?"

"I believe that there are two possibilities. First, as was assumed at the time by many, he lived in the area ... somewhere that was a minute or two from here that he could retreat to before any blood trail was forthcoming."

"I see, and the second?"

"Well, and I am surprised that you did not think of this yourself ... he could have gone under the ground, that is to say used the sewers ... after all, every street has manhole covers leading down to tunnels which would take him any place that he wanted to go unseen, except possibly by the odd rat or two."

Holmes laughed heartily. It told me that very soon both my theories would, indeed, be dismantled with his unfailing logic.

"On your first point it is well made, and as you say it was the assumption of most throughout the investigation. However, as will become clear as we progress, I do not think that the Ripper was a local man or even had an extensive knowledge of the area. For now, though, consider this ... although the killings are called the Whitechapel murders, as you yourself commented we have already walked far from Whitechapel itself, and two out of the remaining three locations are in different areas of the East End. Hence if you did a triangulation of all the murder locations, as I did, it would yield a property in Osborn Street which is not close enough to any of the sites to discount the Ripper from either being observed, or leaving a blood trail right back home. Despite what Assistant Commissioner Anderson asserted about Aaron Kosminski ..."

"That he knew that he was the Ripper, but that the Jewish community would not testify against one of their own," I interjected.

"Exactly, Watson. I would say that in such a circumstance that any group of people, irrespective of their nationality or religion, would want to see justice done and the horrific murders stopped, even if it meant informing on someone they knew. As I mentioned earlier the East End is a group of communities ... Germans, Chinese, French and so on ... and as such they would surely make note of anybody acting in such a suspicious manner as the Ripper? Need I say more than that in the course of the investigation over five thousand good citizens of this district contacted the police with their own ideas and suspects. No, Watson, any Ripper hiding among these people would not last long before being reported."

"If not a local man, then where did he come from?"

"Later, Watson, later ... that is for you to deduce. As for your sewer theory that is quite impossible. In fact, Sir Charles Warren would have known that from the start since he was interested in subterranean tunnels and the like, and even wrote a book on the subject while in Jerusalem, and had a shaft named after him too."

"All very interesting, Holmes, but why is it impossible?"

"For a start the manhole covers are intended to be lifted by two men, and in addition require a special tool. Granted the Ripper may have possessed such an implement, and in his heightened state may have had the strength to lift the cover alone, and so gain entry to the sewer system ... but what would be impossible for him to achieve is the replacing of the cover once he had climbed down through the hole."

"Of course, I see now why that avenue of escape would not be feasible, especially with him having the inconvenience of a bag to carry."

"A bag, Watson, who ever mentioned that he had a bag!"

"Does it not seem logical that he must have had some sort of bag with him, as did you not say earlier that certain body parts were removed from the scene ... parts that would not necessarily fit into a pocket easily."

"Excellent, Watson, excellent."

"Added to that maybe the Ripper had the forethought to provide himself with some spare clothes in order to mitigate any blood splatter."

"I can see that you are thinking of the practicalities involved with committing such crimes. A pity that the detectives at the time were not like you, Watson. Meanwhile returning to your original question, Liverpool Street would present far too many problems for the Ripper to escape unnoticed [38]. A better bet I would say is Bishopsgate station to the north of here, which could be easily accessed by climbing over a wooden gate and descending a flight of steps down to the platform. However, better still would be the prospect of Bishopsgate goods yard, which runs from Shoreditch High Street through to Brick Lane. All the Ripper would need to do is retrace his steps to Brick Lane, for surely that is where he picked up Chapman in the first instance, and follow that road north for approximately two hundred yards."

"Still a risk, but an acceptable one," I commented.

"Are you ready for the next murder, Watson?"

Feeling somewhat pleased with myself, I replied in the affirmative as we set off at a brisk pace, seeking the spot where the body of the Ripper's third victim was found.

Chapter Seven

Elizabeth Stride

As fleet-footed as we were, it was a good fifteen-minutes until we found ourselves to the south of the Commercial Road in Berner Street. It was another drab affair with two long lines of single storey terraced houses, built to a lower standard than those I had seen in Buck's Row earlier that night. Toward the end of the road, close to the junction with Fairclough Street, on the right-hand side one building stood out since it was two-storeys high unlike all the other properties [39]. Between it and the adjoining residence was a gate to Dutfield's Yard and the International Working Men's Educational Club, and it was to this spot at No. 40 Berner Street that Holmes led me.

"The reference book, please, Watson," instructed my friend, just as he had done so at the two previous sites.

I was already prepared for what had become our routine for the investigation, and began to read aloud the facts of the third murder.

"The victim was Elizabeth Stride, maiden name Elizabeth Gustafsdotter, also known as 'Long Liz' possibly on account of her height and long legs. She met her end here at 1.00 a.m. in the yard."

"Somewhat earlier than the others, you may wish to note."

"Indeed. The body was found by the club steward, Louis Diemschutz, who lived on the premises but had been out all day peddling costume jewellery at Crystal Palace. As he drove his cart into the yard, his pony shied to the left and he came across a 'bundle on the ground' by the gateway, which upon inspection was found to be Stride's body. The alarm was raised and soon the police were at the scene. All the club members still present, only around twenty to thirty of them who had remained to drink and sing, were searched and had their statements taken. Others who had been there earlier in the evening were also interviewed, but none had seen a body as late as 12.50 a.m. on the morning in question."

"Note, Watson, that once again, the Ripper had to be a quick worker as there was only a maximum of ten-minutes in which he could commit his act of terror and escape. It is also worth mentioning that there was no light on in the yard so the only possible illumination would have been via the windows of the club next door."

"It would seem to me, Holmes, that the Ripper's *modus operandi* was the same as for Polly Nichols in that he picked up his prey in a main thoroughfare, Commercial Road in this case, and then Stride brought him down here to the relative privacy of Dutfield's Yard. The lack of light would have been an added advantage, and something that Stride may have been aware of from an earlier encounter that night."

"But something that was to the Ripper's advantage as well," commented Holmes. "Now remind me about events leading up to the murder, Watson."

"Stride was seen drinking in the Queen's Head public house, on the corner of Commercial Street and Fashion Street, at around 6.30 p.m. with Elizabeth Tanner, the deputy at the lodging house where she stayed. She was wearing an old black skirt, a black jacket trimmed with fur, and with a posy of a red rose in a spray with either a fern or asparagus leaves pinned to it, a checked neckerchief, and a black crêpe bonnet. There were three possible sightings of her with clients in Berner Street around 11.00 p.m., 11.45 p.m., and 12.45 a.m. respectively."

"Busy lady," commented Holmes.

"The last witness was Israel Schwartz who said that he had seen a man speaking to a woman in the gateway of the club, and that the man had thrown the woman down on to the

64

pavement **[40]**. There was another man across the street lighting a pipe, and when the attacker saw this person he shouted out 'Lipski'. Not wishing to get involved Schwartz ran away from the scene. The second man followed him for a short distance before making his exit."

"I should add at this juncture that Lipski had become a general derogatory term for any Jewish person on account of a pervious murder in Batty Street involving one Israel Lipski, although his actual surname was Lobulsk. He was hanged for the killing of a fellow lodger, Mrs. Miriam Angel, who was pregnant at the time. By coincidence his landlords were a Mr. and Mrs. Lipski. Hence it does not mean that Jack the Ripper, if indeed it was him, knew the man by the lamppost, or, as has been suggested, that the Ripper was of Jewish origin."

"A pity that it is probably a red herring since Schwartz did give a good description of the man with Stride ... he was aged about thirty, around five-foot-five-inches tall with a fair complexion, dark hair, a small brown moustache, full face, and broad shoulders. He was wearing a dark jacket, dark trousers, and a black peak cap, but wasn't carrying anything."

"If this was the Ripper, which I sincerely doubt, then there is the distinct possibility that he was not working alone given that the man by the lamppost could have been a lookout. I suspect that both men did know each other, and that their intention was that of robbing Stride of her night's earnings, but were interrupted by Schwartz walking down the street. The call of Lipski was to alert Mr. Lamppost as to that fact, and direct him to deal with Schwartz ... which he did by pursuing him as far as a nearby railway bridge. Meanwhile the man who had pushed Stride to the ground fled the scene, leaving Stride to return to Commercial Road, and pick up her last gentleman of the night, Jack the Ripper, a few minutes later. She returned with him to Dutfield's Yard, which she had been using all evening as verified by the earlier sightings of her in that vicinity."

"That theory would seem to fit the known facts very nicely, Holmes," I said, with some admiration.

"Naturally. Now you have omitted to mention any details about Stride herself, or when the attack happened."

Hastily I found the relevant information.

"The murder took place on the thirtieth of September ... which before you ask was a Sunday."

"Good, you are learning fast, Watson."

"As to Stride herself she was Swedish by birth, but spoke almost perfect English and Yiddish, was forty-four-years old, had been married to a carpenter named John Stride, and apart from cleaning and other domestic work supplemented her income through prostitution. She had allegedly run a coffee shop in Upper North Street, and later one in Poplar High Street while living with her husband in East India Dock Road. However, after her marriage broke down in 1877, she had been an inmate at the Poplar workhouse before moving to a common lodging house at No. 32 Flower and Dean Street. You made a note in the margin that by all accounts she was prone to fancies, so much of what is reported about her may be false. For example, she claimed to have had nine children, though she is only known to have had one stillborn child in 1865. She also stated that her husband and children had all drowned in the *Princess Alice* disaster of 1878, when, in fact, John Stride was to die of heart disease in Bromley some six years later. More recently she had been living in Devonshire Street with Michael Kidney, a waterside labourer, but seems to have parted company with him since by the twenty-seventh of September 1888 she was back at the common lodging house in Flower and Dean Street."

"There is nothing that can be gleaned from her past history to help us in this case, Watson, but I think you will find the police reports of more interest [41]."

"The police surgeon's report [42] .... Bagster Phillips again I see ... states that 'the body was lying on the near side, with the face turned toward the wall, the head up the yard and the feet toward the street. The left arm was extended and there was a packet of cachous to mask bad breath in the left hand ... The right arm was over the belly; the back of the hand and wrist had on it clotted blood. The legs were drawn up with the feet

66

close to the wall. The body and face were warm and the hand cold. The legs were quite warm ... The throat was deeply gashed, and there was an abrasion of the skin about one-and-a-quarter inches in diameter, apparently stained with blood, under her right brow. ... There was a clear-cut incision on the neck. It was six inches in length and commenced two and a half inches in a straight line below the angle of the jaw, three-quarters of an inch over an undivided muscle, and then, becoming deeper, dividing the sheath. The cut was very clean and deviated a little downwards."

"Any comments?"

"Yes, these injuries, although dreadful, are not as horrific as those of Annie Chapman, and so I conclude that while this is undoubtedly the work of the Ripper, he must have been interrupted this time."

"Well done, Watson. That is the same thinking as the official forces, but then they had another piece of information to help them to their deduction."

"And what was that?"

"Elizabeth Stride was not the only Ripper victim that night."

"So, this is what became known as the 'night of the double event', Holmes."

"Indeed, that is the term the press used to sensationalise the murders, but more importantly it was these two killings that yielded the most clues and an eventual solution for me. Stride was pulled backwards and on to the ground by her neckerchief, the knot of which was tight, before having her throat cut with a single slash as she was pinned there. The knife used, according to the police surgeon, had a shorter blade than that used previously, and it was this detail cojoined with the fact that the location was to the south of Commercial Road, and that the injuries were less severe, that made many conclude that Stride was not a Ripper victim at all. What do you say to that, Watson?"

"Preposterous, Holmes. Elizabeth Stride was most certainly a casualty of the Ripper. The evidence regarding the knife could have been wrong, given that there were not so many incisions upon which to make that deduction, or quite simply the Ripper may have carried more than one such implement with him ... either way it is not a sound conclusion."

"Quite so, but there is a third possibility also ... perhaps the murderer used the victim's own knife. Remember that many women by now secretly arm themselves and carryied a knife for protection against just such an attack. Now, Watson, you know what I am going to ask you next?"

"Yes, the escape route. In this instance as there was a lack of injuries, I would not necessarily expect a blood trail, albeit the Ripper's intention would have been to disfigure Stride in a similar manner to Chapman ... and with this in mind he would have planned his escape most thoroughly. The closest Underground station would be Aldgate East, but that would present a problem since it is no open affair such as Whitechapel and so would be inaccessible to him. I know of no other railway in the area except the tracks of the London, Tilbury & Southend Railway, but the nearest station would be Leman Street ... too far away to avoid the risk of being seen, and in any event entry would not be possible at that hour. I suppose that you are going to tell me that is a suitable goods yard that could have been used."

"Indeed, I am, Watson. The Commercial Road goods yard is only one hundred yards away from the top of Berner Street [43 & 44]. It was built in 1887 with a cobbled roadway leading into a shunting yard, which has ground-level vaults and viaduct-level sidings, a branch line connecting to the aforementioned London, Tilbury and Southend Railway, as well as a goods station below a colossal warehouse. The Ripper could easily have disappeared into that vast complex unnoticed."

"The question still remains as to where the Ripper was going once he had managed to flee the immediate area undetected."

"That will become clearer after we have visited the next location."

"Then are we finished here, Holmes?"

"Yes, let us proceed to Aldgate and where the body of Catherine Eddowes was found later that morning."

Chapter Eight

Catherine Eddowes

As we passed St. Botolph's [45] next to Aldgate Underground station I noted that it had gone 2 a.m., and yet such was my excitement that it did not seem that late at all. The original church Holmes told me dated from the 10th century and belonged to the Knighten Guild and later to the newly established Priory of Holy Trinity. After the dissolution of the monasteries, it fell into disrepair and was reconstructed in 1744. During the building work the body of a boy was found in a standing position, and was put on display with visitors paying 2d. to view him – apparently, according to Holmes, people were very impressed by his well-preserved intestines. Daniel Defoe, author of one of my favourite childhood stories *Robinson Crusoe*, was married here, while the philosopher and social reformer, Jeremy Bentham, was christened in the font.

Adjacent, and part of the churchyard, was the school named after Sir John Cass. It, too, had an interesting history in that it was founded in the 17th century by Sir Samuel Stamp, but by early the following century was in need of money. A benefactor came forward in the form of Alderman Sir John Cass, but he died of a brain haemorrhage, literally as he was about to sign the endowment deed, his body being found with him holding his blood-stained quill, seated at his desk with the unsigned document in front of him. The school was forced to close for nearly ten years until the Chancery saw good sense and enforced the deed. As a result, on Founder's Day every year each pupil is given a pen, stained red, which they wear in their lapel.

"So, yet another beacon to the future, Holmes. As you said earlier East London is indeed a place of growing hope."

"Strictly speaking, in this instance it is not so, Watson, since in the first place the school was not on this site in 1888, and more importantly we have passed over the boundary and are now in the City of London, the rich relative to the orphaned East End."

The next turning on the right brought us to Mitre Square, where Holmes indicated a spot in the southwest corner [46].

"It was here at 1.45 a.m. that the body of Catherine Eddowes was found by Police Constable Edward Watkins."

"The Ripper must have come here immediately after his encounter with Elizabeth Stride, and without any deviation," I commented.

"Precisely, Watson, and that is very much a clue in itself as the Ripper must have made a conscious decision to travel in this direction rather than head, for example, toward Whitechapel where unfortunates upon which to prey would have been more plentiful. I very much suspect that he had something else on his mind having been interrupted earlier, and that Catherine Eddowes was a mere bonus."

"Let me consult your file [47], and I will tell you more about the details of this murder, Holmes."

I thumbed the pages, and in an instant had the relevant facts to convey.

"Catherine Eddowes, like Elizabeth Stride, was also living at a common lodging house in Flower and Dean Street at the time of her murder. Although usually referred to as Eddowes, she also used the surname Kelly after her current partner John Kelly, and sometimes Conway after her ex-partner with whom she had had three children. She was forty-six-years old and one of eleven children herself, and although John Kelly claimed that she was not a prostitute all the evidence points to her being one ... occasional or otherwise ... though both of them had just returned from paid work hop-picking in Kent the previous

Thursday. She was originally from Wolverhampton, and had a reputation for being both cheerful and singing all the time, as well as having a fierce temper. Catherine was just five-feet tall, with dark auburn hair and hazel eyes."

"Move on, Watson, there is nothing here of import. Remind me about her movements just prior to her death."

"Earlier in the day she had told John Kelly that she was going over to see her daughter, Annie Phillips, who lived in Bermondsey, in an attempt to get some money from her since all that she had earned hop-picking had already been spent."

"On drink undoubtedly," commented Holmes.

"It seems that John pawned his boots so that he could afford his place in a common lodging house that night, but you wrote in the margin that you could not verify whether Catherine was successful in obtaining any money from her daughter, or if she even made that journey south of the river. However, at 8.30 p.m. she was found drunk in Aldgate High Street by Police Constable Louis Robinson. Not being able to ascertain where she lived, he, along with another officer, took Eddowes to Bishopsgate police station [48] where she was placed in a cell until she was thought sober enough to leave. That was at around 1.00 a.m. when the police station inspector ordered her to be released. 'Goodnight, old cock,' were her last known words which she said to Police Constable Hutt as she left the station and made her way down Rose Alley to join Bishopsgate."

"They had probably all got tired of her endless singing," speculated Holmes, with a half-smile on his face.

"Here's an inconsistency, Holmes. She gave her name as Mary Ann Kelly along with an address in Fashion Street."

"She simply didn't want her identity and address known in case it went against her the next time she would be in trouble with the police."

"Of course, Holmes. When she left Bishopsgate, she was wearing a black straw bonnet trimmed with green and black velvet, a black cloth jacket with imitation fur, a chintz skirt with a pattern of daisies and golden lilies, a grey stuff petticoat, an old green alpaca skirt, and another even older blue skirt underneath, a neckerchief of red gauze, and an apron. It was noted that she did not go in the direction of Flower and Dean Street, but in the opposite one toward the city."

"Naturally. Remember she had no money for her lodging, so she would need to find a client first. I also recall that it was raining that night."

"Does that make a difference?"

"Possibly .... properties in the city are more expensively build with added refinements such as porches under which to shelter, and even though there might have been less opportunity of finding a client in that area it would at least have been a more comfortable wait. You might even consider that the church of St. Botolph's would make an ideal location in such circumstances."

"You may well be right, Holmes. Her last sighting was at 1.35 a.m. when three men saw her talking with another man, at the entrance to Church Passage, which runs between Mitre Square and Duke Street. A pity that their description of that person, who was almost certainly the Ripper, came to nothing."

"Indeed. What happened once the body was discovered, Watson?"

"There was a tea warehouse in the square, but the night watchman, an ex-police officer himself, said that he had seen and heard nothing, and neither had the night watchman at No. 5, or the off-duty police officer who resided at No. 3."

"And the report of the police surgeon, Watson."

"Ah, that would be Dr. Frederick Gordon Brown who by 2.00 a.m. was at the scene. In his subsequent report **[49]** he stated that, 'the body was on its back, the head turned to her left shoulder. The arms by the side of the body as if they had fallen there ... The clothes drawn up above the abdomen. The thighs were naked ... The throat cut across ... below the throat was a neckerchief ... The intestines were drawn out to a large extent and placed over the right shoulder ... they were smeared over with some feculent matter. A piece of about two feet was quite detached from the body and placed between the body and the left arm, apparently by design. The lobe and auricle of the right ear were cut obliquely through. There was a quantity of clotted blood on the pavement on the left side of the neck round the shoulder and upper part of the arm, and fluid blood-coloured serum which had flowed under the neck to the right shoulder, the pavement sloping in that direction ... The peritoneal lining was cut through on the left side and the left kidney carefully taken out and removed."

"There can be no room for dissent that this was another Ripper victim. Now to the weapon used, Watson ... was it a six-inch blade as with Nichols and Chapman, or a shorter one as was said to be employed for Stride?"

"Six-inches, Holmes, meaning that it was most likely that the police surgeon made a mistake regarding the implement used for Stride."

"I agree, Watson, but do read on as you will find that there was soon to be a major disagreement between the professionals involved."

I did as was instructed.

"Hmm, at first it was believed that the perpetrator of the act must have had considerable experience of the position of the organs in the abdominal cavity and the way of extracting them ... 'It required a great deal of knowledge to have removed the kidney and to know where it was placed. Such a knowledge might be possessed by one in the habit of cutting up animals. I think the perpetrator of this act had sufficient time ... It would take at least five minutes. ... I believe it was the act of one person'."

I paused before continuing as I had reached the end of the page.

"That seems pretty conclusive, Holmes, and certainly points to a 'Leather Apron' as speculated earlier."

However, as I turned to a new leaf there were further statements upon this point.

"Now I see what you mean, Holmes, for it says here that later Dr. Thomas Bond, the police physician, was to disagree as to the murderer's skill level. He stated that, 'in each case the mutilation was inflicted by a person who had no scientific nor anatomical knowledge. In my opinion he does not even possess the technical knowledge of a butcher or horse slaughterer or any person accustomed to cut up dead animals'. Dr. William Saunders, the Public Analyst for the City of London, agreed in that he believed that the Ripper was not looking for any particular organ, and just happened upon those removed which were cut out with no significant anatomical skill."

"So, my friend, you are a doctor ... tell me, in your opinion, who is correct."

"I cannot possibly speculate on such a matter without seeing the evidence, but it is two to one against 'Leather Apron'."

"Let me guide you a little. I am sure that as a medical man you could have easily inflicted all the injuries thus far seen, and removed the organs stated without any trouble ... but could you have done so with the victim laying on a pavement, in the cold, and in more than one instance in wet weather?"

"More difficult, but I have been called upon to perform surgery on the field of battle, so yes I could certainly do it."

"And do it in just a few minutes?"

"In those conditions you are under fire, and so, again, yes I could do it in just a few seconds if required."

"But could you do it blindfolded, Watson?"

"Of course not, Holmes, don't be so absurd."

"Well, the Ripper might as well have been blindfolded for let us not forget that Dutfield's Yard had no light, nor did the yard at the back of No. 29 Hanbury Street, the whole of Buck's Row at the time had but one lamppost, and I note that this dark corner of Mitre Square still after all these years has no decent light by which to perform such surgery either ... on the night in question the closest lamppost was twenty-five yards away. Need I say more?"

"Brilliant, Holmes. Saunders and Bond were not considering the conditions under which the mutilations took place."

"Let me take you one step further to consolidate my proposition."

At this Holmes called out to a fellow who was loafing at the far side of the square. He took out a sovereign from his waistcoat pocket and said, "This is for you, if you can show me where your kidneys are located."

The man laughed and pointed to where his lungs were positioned.

"Excellent. And where is your heart?"

This time the man got it almost correct, but when Holmes finally asked him to indicate the location of his liver, he looked rather blank and pointed vaguely to his stomach. It was clear by now that he had little knowledge of anatomy.

"Well done. You have earned this coin ... don't spend it all on alcohol," advised Holmes, as the man scurried off with the easiest money he would ever earn.

"Yes, of course, we are well educated men who know of such things, whereas the general public have no idea about their body, or how it all fits together."

"And under what category is the Ripper would you estimate, Watson?"

"Not a highly educated individual, but one with enough knowledge to be able to perform this rough surgery ... so he must have had some anatomical knowledge ... somebody who works in butchery would be just about right, Holmes."

"The very same conclusion as myself, Watson."

"How did this Dr. Saunders become involved in the case anyway, Holmes?"

"Because as I indicated earlier, this is the first, and only, Ripper murder to take place within the confines of the City of London ... and that is of crucial importance as you will learn later."

"Does that mean that Eddowes was investigated by a different police force? That could lead to confusion at many levels could it not?"

"Actually, it helped greatly since it became a joint investigation, and was to result in the production of some excellent crime scene drawings and plans of the vicinity. The newspapers still remained hostile as they simply did not appreciate the amount of work that was involved. Chief Inspector Swanson reported that eighty-thousand leaflets appealing for information regarding Elizabeth Stride's death were circulated, and that in just one strand of that investigation some two-thousand lodgers were interviewed and their statements taken. Imagine the amount of work that would entail, especially since as we both know witness statements often contradict each other."

I contemplated what Holmes had just imparted before returning to something that had been bothering me ever since we had departed Berner Street.

"After the Stride murder, we left the Ripper fleeing the scene via the Commercial Road goods yard, so how did he get from there to here?"

"Actually, Watson, there is a way he could do it with little chance of being seen **[50]**. From the Commercial Road depot, he could gain access to the sidings which are a spur from the London, Tilbury and Southend Railway. If when he reached the main line, he turned toward the terminus at Fenchurch Street there is another branch line just past Leman Street station which ends at the Hayden Square goods yard, which you might have noticed earlier if you had been looking immediately opposite Aldgate Underground station, and not at the more ornate St. Botolph's."

I shrugged my shoulders as I had not observed it.

"Never mind. I assure you that it exists, and although on elevated tracks it would have been more than possible for the Ripper to exit, for such places are designed to keep intruders out, not in. Back in 1888, I made the journey myself, and can vouch that it can be done at leisure in around thirty-minutes, so there was ample time for the Ripper to make the journey from Berner Street to Aldgate undetected, and then to pick up Eddowes."

"You said earlier that the second victim that evening was not intended originally."

"I did."

"In that case why did he come here in the first place, and not make off in a different, and perhaps less hazardous, direction?"

"Can you not deduce that for yourself, Watson?"

"Because he needed to reach an open Underground station, and Aldgate was the nearest," I speculated, with some hesitation.

"Quite so ... but how did you know that Aldgate is an open station, Watson?"

"Simple, Holmes .... I employed my memory. Do not forget that we both visited that station, for it is where the unfortunate body of Cadogan-West, late employee of Woolwich Arsenal, ended up beside the tracks. You might recall that I published that affair under the title of *The Adventure of the Bruce-Partington Plans.*"

"One of your better efforts at recording our cases, I always thought," said Holmes, with just a hint of sarcasm.

"Let me add something further then?" said I. "You have been very keen on mentioning the lack of a blood trail thus far. Well, in the thirty or so minutes it would take to travel here from Berner Street any blood splatter on the Ripper's clothing, which would have been limited given that his mutilation of Stride was interrupted, would have congealed. It is also possible that he may have changed his outer garments."

"Yes, I agree."

"But the murder of Eddowes, according to the report, resulted in much fresh blood, and as a consequence almost certainly a trail to follow, so why was it missed yet again?"

"Are you not forgetting something, Watson?"

"I cannot think of anything."

"It was raining ..."

"And so, any evidence of blood would have simply been washed away by the time the official forces were on the scene. Is there anything else to be discovered here, Holmes," said I, a little exasperated that my efforts in deduction were leading nowhere fast.

"Not here precisely but close by, if you would care to follow me. You see, as well as a kidney being removed by the Ripper, probably as a trophy, a piece of Eddowes's apron was also found to be missing."

"If he had the kidney, why would he also want something as insignificant as part of her apron? He might take the whole garment perhaps, but not just a portion."

"In this instance, my friend, I can only speculate. Perhaps he used that part of the apron to wrap the kidney, and then had no need of it later once he either transferred it to his bag, if he ever had one, or had eaten it."

"Holmes, you cannot be serious."

"It is a distinct possibility, since of all the said sightings of the Ripper almost none of them ever mentions a person carrying a bag, though we both agree that one would have been useful. Conversely, as you will learn later, there was a correspondence from the Ripper, thought to be genuine at the time, in which he states that he had eaten the said organ for breakfast, albeit that he had cooked it first."

"Surely we are not dealing with some sort of a vampire, werewolf, or cannibal, Holmes?"

"No, I think not, but just in case it was somebody with such delusions, I did check the lunar calendar for each of the murders. It transpired that the phases were all different with never a full or half moon, so I feel that we can discount such a scenario."

Holmes paused to allow that fact to take hold, before making his final comment as we left Mitre Square.

"I can only say that the Ripper discarded the portion of apron he took, and that shortly afterward at 3.00 a.m. Police Constable Alfred Long found it, stained with blood and faecal matter, lying in the passage of a doorway at the Model Dwellings in Goulston Street .... and what is more there was something else to accompany it!"

Chapter Nine

The Writing on the Wall

Back past St. Botolph's and Aldgate Underground station, over the major thoroughfare of Middlesex Street, and then next left brought us to Goulston Street, which although quiet now would spring to life with market stalls each Sunday morning **[51]**. The area had been renowned as the centre for clothes manufacturing ever since the arrival of the Huguenots in the 1600s, and although Middlesex Street had been around since the 1830s, many a local would still refer to it, and its environs, as Petticoat Lane. The buildings were in the main all three and four-storeys tall comprising of flats on the upper floors, and shops on the ground floor. Each shop it seemed had an extendable coloured awning which when out on a fine summer's day would present a most pleasant sight for the passer-by, and certainly a long cry from the alleys and slums that predominated here prior to the clearances of the early 1880s. The Goulston Street Improvement, as it was called at the time, had led to the building of Model Dwellings **[52]** that opened in 1887 and contained two-hundred-and-twenty-two residences, which by the time of the Ripper were inhabited almost exclusively by Jewish families, who now dominated the whole of this part of the East End. It was to those Model Dwellings and the passage leading to Nos. 108 and 119 **[53]** that Holmes led me.

"This is it, Watson. If you look at the Ripper File it will tell you what else, apart from the portion of apron, was found

79

here ... and hopefully you will be able to make your own deductions?"

In fact, I was already aware of the discovery heralded in certain circles as the Goulston Street graffito, but decided to play along with Holmes, for sometimes I found it best to pander to his ego. Hence, I thumbed through the volume until I found the relevant pages, and then read to Holmes the pertinent facts, while pretending to be surprised by them.

"Above the apron on the wall, and in chalk, were the words, 'The Juwes are The men that Will not be Blamed for nothing' written over five lines [54]. However, it was not to remain there for long as on the orders of Sir Charles Warren [55], at the suggestion of Police Superintendent Thomas Arnold [56], the graffito was washed away before it could be photographed. The reason given was that with dawn approaching the police did not want to incite a riot in this mainly Jewish district, especially at a time when tensions were at a peak."

I paused for effect before adding my disgust in a raised voice.

"That's scandalous, Holmes."

"No, Watson, it was desirable ... it was the most sensible course of action. Remember it was a Sunday morning and soon this street would be a throng of market traders, mainly Jewish, who would no doubt react badly to such words directed at them, however bad the spelling."

"But the writing itself brings several questions to mind ..."

"Yes, it is curious, but before we delve into that thread, I think it would be better if first you finish reading the rest of the entry for Eddowes regarding the subsequent official police investigation."

"If you think it best, Holmes. It says here that by the second of October the police had pieced together from various interviews a general description of the Ripper as being 'of shabby appearance, about thirty-years of age and five-feet-nine-inches in height, of fair complexion, having a small fair moustache, and a cap with a peak'."

"Apart from his height it concurs with the description given by Israel Schwartz, but contradicts those of other witnesses given during the course of the investigation," commented Holmes.

"The newspapers continued their criticism of the police efforts [57], and the general public flooded the police with letters suggesting lines of enquiry that might be taken. Among the suggestions were that the Ripper disguised himself as a policeman, that a gang might be responsible, that the murderer was a watchman, and so on ..."

"All were well-intentioned, and some with sound ideas."

"You even made a note that Sir Arthur Conan Doyle, our literary agent, was consulted by the police. He apparently came to the conclusion that Jack the Ripper was really Jill the Ripper.[1]"

"Yes, I know ... absolute nonsense, albeit well-meaning."

"It just goes to show the desperation of the official force in that they even contemplated asking an amateur."

"And let's not forget the plethora of fake letters that were received in the name of Jack the Ripper ever since the publication of the 'Dear Boss' letter, purportedly written on the twenty-fifth of September some days before the night of the double event, but not forwarded to the police until the eve of that atrocity, and published afterwards. Each communication had to be investigated in order to be eliminated, and this just took up more valuable police time and resources."

"There is mention here of one known as the 'Saucy Jack' postcard [58 & 59] sent on the first of October which gave details of the double event. Many thought that it might be genuine."

Holmes laughed.

"It was not for one very good reason."

"And what was that?"

"Presumably the intention of the 'Saucy Jack' postcard, if from the Ripper, was to establish his credentials with some

---

[1] The only evidence for this assertion comes from Sir Arthurs's son, Adrian Conan Doyle, who many years after the event stated that his father thought it 'likely that the man had a rough knowledge of surgery and probably clothed himself as a woman to avoid undue attention by the police and to approach his victims without arousing suspicion on their part'. He certainly did not entertain the proposition that the murderer was female.

piece of knowledge not generally known. To this end it mentioned that he had no time to 'get the ears for police', but on the same day as it was posted *The Telegraph* had already reported that the injuries included a 'gash extended to the right ear, which was sliced off' so this postcard added nothing new. What the postcard should have mentioned, and what was not made public until the first session of the inquest on the fifth of October was that the left kidney was also missing."

"Wait a minute, Holmes … there was another letter which did mention the kidney, I am sure."

"Indeed, there was, and not just a letter but half a preserved kidney as well. The package was sent to George Lusk, the chairman of the Whitechapel Vigilance Committee. It contained a letter alleged to be 'From Hell' **[60]** with the writer claiming that he had fried and eaten the other half of the kidney, which was 'very nise'. At first it was thought that the letter was genuine for the kidney did match the one missing from Eddowes's body in that it had the correct length of renal artery where it had been severed, and had Bright's disease."

"Alcoholism was very common among the unfortunate community, and consequently, as a direct result, so was Bright's disease."

"I was suspicious immediately as the package was not received until the sixteenth of October by which time it was common knowledge that a kidney had been removed. It transpired that I was fully justified for later evidence showed that the kidney had been trimmed, the renal artery was entirely absent, and it had been placed in preservative. The original conclusion changed to the kidney having been obtained from a hospital mortuary and sent, most likely, by a medical student as some sort of sick joke. Furthermore, if ever Inspector Lestrade had examined the document closely it would have been evident, even to him, that it was written by an educated person trying to give the impression of being an illiterate one."

"So, are you saying that of all the letters sent not a single one was from the Ripper?"

"That is exactly so, Watson. The Ripper did not seek the notoriety that the press gave him, and, indeed, he did not want to give any clues that might help the official forces capture him."

"Following your hypothesis then the graffito must also be a fake, Holmes?"

"Not quite a fake for it certainly existed, but I am pretty certain that it was not written by the Ripper. You see the graffito and the various pieces of written correspondence act as counterpoints for each other."

"I don't understand," said I, genuinely confused by this statement.

"Then let me explain. If you accept that the Ripper wrote the graffito with its single mistake of 'Juwes', and compare it to any of his supposed letters, then those documents cannot be genuine since they are written in a different style, and with many more errors in grammar and spelling. Conversely if you regard any of the correspondence being in the hand of the Ripper, then for the converse reasons the graffito cannot be authentic."

"That only eliminates one or other, but not both sets of possible evidence, Holmes," said I, thinking that I had found a flaw in my friend's reasoning.

"A fair comment. Let us suppose for the moment that the writing on the wall is genuine. After all we know that the Ripper was at least by the graffito, since it was also where the portion of apron was discovered, and given that both appeared at the same time according to Police Constable Long who passed the spot and noted nothing thirty minutes earlier it would be logical to assume, for now at least, that both are connected. Analyse the text and tell me what you can deduce from it, Watson?"

"Supposing that the Ripper was the author of those words, then assuming that he meant 'Jews' by 'Juwes', why are they the ones that will not be blamed for nothing? He is inferring that they will be blamed for something, and it must be the murder of the four unfortunates. However, none of the victims were Jewish, so maybe he is actually indicating that he was Jewish himself?"

"Excellent, Watson. That is certainly the inference, but why would the Ripper give away such a clue when, as I have just established, he wanted no publicity, and no clues as to his identity revealed?"

"It does not seem logical," I confessed.

"In addition why is it only now that the Ripper begins to write messages on walls to aid, or mislead, the police? Surely if it were him, then he would have placed it closer to the body, most likely on the pavement, or a convenient wall, next to the corpse, but not several streets away where it might never be seen. Furthermore, why would the Ripper be carrying chalk in his pocket anyway, there is nothing to suggest that he was a teacher, tailor or even an artist who might legitimately carry chalk around with him. If he felt the need to leave such a message now, why had he not done so before, or with the murder yet to come?"

"You put forward a strong case, but if not the Ripper, then who?"

"I don't know, and I'm not sure that it is especially pertinent to the case. Maybe it was written by one of those good-intentioned persons who had seen something they regarded as important. Perhaps they had written to the police about it and, having been ignored, decided to make a more public statement. In this scenario the person is most definitely pointing the finger at the Ripper as being of Jewish origin, or the Jewish community being responsible for shielding the fiend. I would even go as far to suggest that they believed that the culprit lived here in the Model Dwellings in one of the flats between No. 108 and 119, otherwise why hide the graffito in this passageway? Surely, it would have been better to display it in a more prominent place where it would be seen by the masses?"

"That's incredible, Holmes. Do you really think that might be possible, or are you still convinced that the Ripper was not local to the area?"

"I am still of the opinion that the Ripper was not a resident of the East End. If you wanted to find the person who wrote

84

that message you could do worse than look for somebody who is a sailor, and who hails originally from the Baltic."

"Why, Holmes?"

"As you have rightly pointed out only the word 'Juwes' is spelt wrongly. Does that not seem strange to you, Watson?"

"It does."

"Well then, suppose that the spelling is actually correct … if so, several options presented themselves. First, and least likely, in Lithuanian the word 'Juwes' exists and translates as jewel, but that would make no sense in the context of the message. However, although in German the word for Jew is 'Juden', in Middle Low German, a development of Old Saxon which died out in the Middle Ages, the word for Jew was 'Juwe'. This form of German was prevalent along the Baltic coast, and used extensively by sailors. It could just be that an ex-sailor from Germany, now residing in the East End, slipped back into this all but extinct spelling. Of course, another explanation of the graffito could be that it relates not to the murders at all, but to some local dispute with a family by the name, or nickname, of 'Juwes', or something similar. I chose not to waste further time on the true interpretation of the graffito since I regarded it to be a red herring."

"But what about the fact that Police Constable Long stated that it was not present prior to the portion of apron being found?"

"I believe that the officer was mistaken. The graffito was there earlier but was simply not spotted as Police Constable Long was not looking for it *per se*. The use of chalk for the writing of slogans, advertising of products, personal messages, and the making of religious and political points was quite common at the time and so would have gone largely unnoticed. Furthermore, it would be difficult to spot chalk writing on a wall at night in a dimly lit street at the best of times, let along on the jamb of a doorway as in this case. Depending on whether it was the right or left jamb, and in which direction Police Constable Long was passing earlier it might well have been out of view, whereas a piece of cloth on the ground would certainly attract his attention. What is more important is how the Ripper came to be in that passageway in the first place. Perhaps you would like to attempt to reconstruct the Ripper's movements from the time he left Hayden Square goods yard **[61]**, Watson?"

"It would seem to me that if as you say, Holmes, that the Ripper walked along the tracks from the goods yard at Commercial Road to the one at Hayden Square, that over that time his heightened state would have subsided, and his blood pressure and heart rate would have returned to near normal. He would also have had time to tend to his general appearance so that, as he emerged into Aldgate High Street, he would not look suspicious in the least, and would be taken for a worker on his way home after the night shift. Close to the church steps I even noticed a water fountain **[62]** in which he might have washed his hands and face of any blood."

"Superlative, Watson. You may have missed the goods yard, but not that clue. Do continue."

"His intention would have been to gain access to the open station of Aldgate, but this plan was modified upon him seeing Eddowes soliciting for trade in the vicinity. On her part she would have regarded the Ripper as just another client, and taken him to the quietest spot she knew, that being Mitre Square. It was badly lit, and she may have even been aware that it was one of the few locations in the area that was subject to a single-police beat, meaning that an officer would only pass by the square every thirty minutes or so. The Ripper did his work with his usual quick efficiency, and then would have presumably made for Aldgate Underground station. Why he did not go there I cannot say, Holmes."

"As far as it goes, Watson, an excellent account of what without doubt happened. I believe that the Ripper did go in the direction of Aldgate, but had to change his plans when it became clear that he would be seen. Perhaps he heard footsteps, or saw a policeman approaching. He could not turn back the way he came as very soon he knew that Eddowes's body would be discovered, and that the place would be swarming with police. His only logical option was to continue along Aldgate High Street and return when he thought the person, or persons, blocking his escape route would have moved on. The first road he would have encountered is Middlesex Street, a major thoroughfare so that would not be an option for him, but the next on the left is Goulston Street, a much narrower and quieter road altogether at that time of day."

"The passageway of the Model Dwellings was perhaps chosen when he noticed the graffito on the wall."

"Possibly, but by now he would have been be panicking for he knew that he had only minutes before the alarm would be raised, and after that his chances of escape unseen would be severely diminished. In the shelter of the passageway, maybe because it was also raining, he could continue to clean himself up as best he could, and so he resorted to using the piece of apron in which he had wrapped the kidney, which he subsequently discarded. I very much doubt if he cared that it might be found, or that when cojoined with the graffito that it would produce a clue so misleading that there would be speculation about it for years to come. In his renewed state of anxiety, he might not have even noticed the graffito in the first instance, or if he did it is quite possible that he did not recognise the significance of it."

"And when he unwrapped the kidney, did he eat it, or place it back in his pocket or bag, Holmes?"

"Not relevant, Watson, as it makes no difference to the outcome. What I do know is that the Ripper was lucky in not being detected on this occasion, for he was able to return to Aldgate a few minutes later and to disappear on to the railway tracks just as before."

"I can understand that getting into a goods yard is fairly easy, but how would he gain admission to the station? I looked earlier as we passed and the drop down to the tracks is considerable [63], and there are locked gates barring entrance via the booking hall."

"Well observed, Watson. However, when rebuffed at the front door it is always worth trying the side entrance. In this case Blue Boar Alley [64] runs down the east side of the station with a wall of only around ten feet high, the other side of which are the flat roofs of the station offices [65] from which the platforms would be accessible without any trouble."

"Earlier, Holmes you inferred a fifth Ripper victim …"

"Indeed, I did and it is high time that we made for that location," said he, striding off in the general direction of Spitalfields.

Chapter Ten

Mary Kelly

As we walked the empty byways of the East End from Goulston Street, across Wentworth Street into Bell Lane, on into Crispin Street, and finally right into Dorset Street, I read ahead so that I would be fully prepared for any questions that Holmes might pose.

"The final murder took place on Friday the ninth of November, over a month later ... is that significant in itself, Holmes?"

The consulting detective made no comment, so I continued my narrative.

"In the weeks that followed the double event the police continued their investigations much as before, only with even more men at their disposal. More leaflets were printed, a reward of £500 was now offered from the City of London Corporation, there were other offers of rewards, too, but not by the police. The two police forces held daily meetings, various properties were searched, arrests made, suspects interviewed and then released, police patrols were stepped up to a frequency of every fifteen minutes, and even two bloodhounds, Barnaby and Burgho [66], were assessed over a two-day period in Regent's Park and Hyde Park respectively for their ability to follow a scent should another murder occur."

"And did any of this convince the press that the police were investigating as best they could?"

I sighed.

"No, the newspapers were now even more critical of the official force, running headlines such as *The Headless Criminal Investigation Department* and *Why Detectives Don't Detect* [67]. Some four-thousand women signed a petition to Queen Victoria, and the police received a further one-thousand-five-hundred letters of help along with some confessions. In fact, such was the general fascination with Jack the Ripper that Mitre Square, in particular, was becoming a tourist attraction with sightseers wanting to view where the murder took place."

"Bizarre, I know, but I suspect that a hundred years from now people will still be taking tours of Whitechapel just to view the murder sites."

"Oh, I think that is an exaggeration, Holmes. I note that you have a transcript of a letter written on the twenty-third of October 1888 to the Home Secretary, Robert Anderson, who was by then also the head of the Criminal Investigation Department as well as being the Assistant Commissioner, in which he expresses his frustration in general ... 'I wish to guard against its being supposed that the inquiry is now concluded ... that a crime of this kind should have been committed without any clue being supplied by the criminal, is unusual, but that five successive murders should have been committed without our having the slightest clue of any kind is extraordinary, if not unique, in the annals of crime. The result has been to necessitate our giving attention to innumerable suggestions, such as would in any ordinary case be dismissed unnoticed ... moreover, the activity of the police has been to a considerable extent wasted through the exigencies of sensational journalism, and the action of unprincipled persons, who, from various motives, have endeavoured to mislead us. But on the other hand, the public generally, and especially the inhabitants of the East End, have shown a remarkable desire to assist in every way, even at some sacrifice to themselves ... the vigilance of the officers engaged on the inquiry continues unabated'."

"I kept it because it demonstrates the difficulties that faced the official forces, and not least of all because it was shortly after this letter was written that I was approached to add my own expertise to the investigation."

"Ah, enter Sherlock Holmes pursued by a Ripper!" said I, with some allusion to *A Winter's Tale*.

"Yes, Watson, but I think that your humour will change when you read the next section about the gruesome circumstances surrounding Mary Jane Kelly who was slaughtered, and I choose my words carefully, inside her single room at No. 13 Miller's Court **[68]** just behind where we now stand outside No. 26 Dorset Street **[69 &70]**."

"Do not worry about me, Holmes, I have already looked ahead and seen the two crime scenes photographs **[71 & 72]** you pasted into your file, and they are indeed horrific. I have also noted that it was once more Dr. Bond and Dr. Phillips who jointly examined the body this time, with the latter suggesting that such mutilations would have taken the Ripper some two hours to complete, though he did not believe that the person responsible showed any sign of either medical or anatomical training. Again, they came to the conclusion that a knife with a six-inch blade was used."

"Just for completeness, do remind me of the injuries sustained by Kelly."

"They were, as you say, most gruesome. 'The body was lying naked in the middle of the bed ... the legs were wide apart, the left thigh at right angles to the trunk and the right forming an obtuse angle with the pubis. The whole of the surface of the abdomen and thighs was removed and the abdominal cavity emptied of its viscera. The breasts were cut off, the arms mutilated by several jagged wounds and the face hacked beyond recognition of the features. The tissues of the neck were severed all round down to the bone. The viscera were found in various parts viz. the uterus and kidneys with one breast under the head, the other breast by the right foot, the liver between the feet, the intestines by the right side and the spleen by the left side of the body. The flaps removed from the abdomen and thighs were on a table. The bed clothing at the right corner was saturated with blood, and on the floor beneath was a pool of blood covering about two feet square ... The face was gashed in all directions, the nose, cheeks, eyebrows, and ears being partly removed. The lips were blanched and cut by several incisions running obliquely down to the chin. There were also numerous cuts extending irregularly across all the features ... Both breasts were more or less removed by circular incisions, the muscle down to the ribs being attached to the breasts ...'. In fact, unlike the other victims, it was remarked that Kelly's body had not been ripped open, but sliced."

"Yes, there were many features of this killing which were singular, Watson."

"For a start I can see from another illustration that she was quite a pretty girl, and much younger than the other victims [73]."

"Quite so. She was just twenty-five."

"She seems to have been a woman of some mystery since she also went by the names Marie Jeanette, 'Fair' Emma, 'Ginger', 'Dark' Mary, and 'Black' Mary. Irish by descent, being born most probably in Limerick, but just like Elizabeth Stride was prone to flights of fantasy. Hence, you wrote that she may, or may not, have lived in Wales, where she married a coal miner named Davis or Davies, been disowned by her parents, come from a moderately wealthy family, had seven brothers and a sister, had a family member on the London theatrical stage, been well educated, and a good artist."

"Nothing particularly relevant thus far ... do continue, Watson, I am getting bored."

"She was reported as being a blonde, or a redhead, which rather contradicts her being known as 'Black' Mary, or 'Ginger'. Kelly was five-feet-seven-inches in height, slim, attractive, and with a fresh complexion." I paused for a moment. "Ah, now I understand, the 'Dark' Mary title comes from the fact that while resident in the East End she took to drinking heavily, after which she would start to sing Irish songs, and become generally abusive and unpleasant."

"Yes, Watson, all very interesting, but nothing of relevance to our investigation."

I could tell that Holmes was getting fractious, probably as a result of the cold combined with the early hour, an hour at which any sane person would be in the arms of Morpheus. However, I was not to be deterred, so I continued with some more background information regarding victim number five.

"It seems that in approximately 1884 she moved to London and worked in Chelsea, and Fitzrovia, where she became a high-class prostitute working out of a brothel. Being young and attractive she was very popular, and one client even took her to France. It was after this that she adopted the French name Marie Jeanette."

"So, what brought her here to the very depths of human existence, Watson?"

"It doesn't say, but there was most assuredly a downturn in her life, for a year later she was to be found in the East End, lodging in the Ratcliffe Highway, and later in Stepney, before ending up at a lodging house in Thrawl Street, just around the corner from here. It was there that she met, and became partner to, a fish porter at Billingsgate market called Joseph Barnett ..."

"Remember him from earlier, Watson? He was one of the more credible suspects."

"I do, but you discounted him most correctly. Either way they lived together in George Street, then Little Paternoster Row, followed by a period in Brick Lane, before finally settling in Dorset Street in early 1888. At the time of her murder, they were not together, having argued a week before about Kelly letting other prostitutes use their dwelling. Add to that there was also friction between them, because Barnett had recently lost his job, so forcing Kelly back onto the streets."

"Yes, Watson. Life can be cruel even to those who try their best ... it is a sobering thought for us all, don't you think?"

I nodded in assent.

"Now, relate the circumstances on the night of her demise."

"It was raining hard when Barnett visited Kelly at Miller's Court at around 7.00 p.m. ... he found her with an unfortunate named Maria Harvey, and soon they were joined by another, Lizzie Albrook, before Barnett and Harvey left together. At that hour Kelly was sober, but later in the evening she was seen in the company of Elizabeth Foster at The Ten Bells on the corner of Commercial Street and Fournier Street, and later still with two other people at The Horn of Plenty in Dorset Street. By the time she returned to Miller's Court with a man at 11.45 p.m., being spotted by another unfortunate called Mary Cox, who resided at No. 5 Miller's Court, she was most certainly drunk."

I paused as a thought came to me.

"If that man was the Ripper, Holmes, then it was significantly earlier than all the other murders."

"Read on," said Holmes, "and you will answer your own question."

"Ah, I now see that there were other sightings of Kelly later that night. Apparently, she could be heard singing in her room as late as 1.00 a.m., but by 1.30 a.m. the singing, according to Elizabeth Prater who lived directly above, had stopped. At 2.00 a.m. Kelly was spotted by a man named George Hutchinson who stated that he met her in Flower and Dean Street, after which she went off in the direction of Thrawl Street where she was approached by a wealthy-looking man of Jewish appearance. Hutchinson was suspicious of this person who looked so out of place in the area. Consequently, he kept watch on them both until 2.45 a.m. at which point they had been inside No. 13 Miller's Court for some time. Sarah Lewis, at No. 2 Miller's Court, was able to partially verify these latter movements, as she confirmed seeing a drunk man and women at 2.30 a.m. in the courtyard. Crucially, Prater and Lewis both heard a faint cry of 'Murder' between 3.30 a.m. and 4.00 a.m., but had taken no notice of it at the time since such cries were commonplace in the area. Finally, Cox reported that she had heard somebody leaving Kelly's room at 5.45 a.m."

"It would seem that she picked up the Ripper in Thawl Street, and by 2.30 a.m. had returned with him to her room. She was murdered at approximately 3.30 a.m., and with the mutilations taking around two hours to complete the Ripper was not able to leave until 5.45 a.m. as confirmed by Cox."

"And, of course, his escape route did not matter this time since he had been indoors with ample time to commit the deed, and then to clean himself off before being seen in public again."

"In fact, the body was not discovered until 10.45 a.m., and only then when Kelly's landlord, John McCarthy, sent his assistant, Thomas Bowyer, around to collect some six-weeks of rent arrears, which might explain why she had been out soliciting in the atrocious weather the night before. He knocked on the door and there was no answer. Ordinarily, he would have gone away, if it had not been for a broken pane of glass through which he could put his hand and push aside the clothing covering it in order to see if the room was occupied."

"What a terrible shock he must have had to view such horror in front of him. A sight to haunt him the rest of his days," I commented.

"Indeed. In fact, John McCarthy later stated that 'the sight looked like the work of the devil'. Meanwhile let me direct you to two important points to remember for later, Watson. First it had been raining all night, and was still raining that morning, and second, that it was the day of the Lord Mayor's show."

I noted both comments, but as I could not conjecture their significance, I continued reading aloud extracts from Holmes's book concerning the subsequent police investigation [74].

"The police were called and were soon on the scene. Among them were Police Superintendent Thomas Arnold, Detective Inspector Edmund Reid [75], Detective Inspector Frederick Abberline [76], and Assistant Commissioner Robert Anderson. The bloodhounds Barnaby and Burgho were called for, but to no avail since they had already been sent back to their owner's in Scarborough. It was noted that women's clothes had been burnt in the fireplace, presumably to give more light for the Ripper to carry out his mutilations, since the only other form of light in the room was a single candle. News travelled fast and it is estimated one-thousand people soon gathered in Dorset Street, with many of them voicing their disapproval at the police. The official investigation included extensive questioning of both Barnett and Hutchinson, as well as door-to-door searches. A pardon was even offered for anybody who might be considered an accomplice, if they came forward with the identity of the Ripper. Sir Charles Warren was also to resign, not over the Whitechapel murders *per se* but over articles he had written attacking government interference in what he considered were police matters."

"That was a great pity, Watson. As I have already said he was a good man, and although he was disliked by the press and the politicians, he was respected by his own men, with virtually every police superintendent on the force visiting him at home to express their support, and regret at his departure."

"The inquest at Shoreditch Town Hall produced no new evidence, though in his report Dr. Bond did give a profile of the type of person the police were looking for as being 'quite likely an inoffensive looking man, probably middle-aged, and neatly and respectably dressed. I think he must be in the habit of wearing a cloak, or overcoat, or he could hardly have escaped notice in the streets if the blood on his hands and clothes were visible'."

"The idiot, Watson! He probably did more harm to the investigation than any other individual ... he gave the public that ludicrous image of Jack the Ripper as being a gentleman with a top hat, cloak, and cane as if attending the opera."

"Well, at least he didn't have him in a deerstalker, and Ulster coat," said I, trying to lighten the mood. "In his defence he was just about the only person to make mention of the Ripper having blood about his person, and he did say that the perpetrator was most likely a solitary, eccentric individual who was subject to periodic attacks of homicidal and erotic mania, who had been in an extreme state of satyriasis as he performed his mutilations."

"After five murders I feel it was a little late for him to state the obvious."

"I agree, Holmes. In fact, Queen Victoria made a more incisive statement in her letter to the Prime Minister when she wrote, 'This new most ghastly murder shows the absolute necessity for some very decided action. All these courts must be lit, and our detectives improved. They are not what they should be. You promised, when the first murder took place, to consult with your colleagues about it'. And that was it I suppose ... Mary Kelly was the last victim so after her demise the official investigation could end."

"Not so, Watson ... in fact, the reverse. There were one-hundred-and-forty-three plain-clothes officers involved in the investigation in the November and December of 1888, that is one-hundred more than in the September. Taking in all ranks the Whitechapel Division had nearly six-hundred men on which to call. It was only in the New Year that the investigation was wound down. Somewhere there you will have the end of year report from James Monro [77], who had taken over as Commissioner after the resignation of Sir Charles Warren … do read it to me as it is summarises the situation perfectly."

It was easily found.

"He stated that 'the murders in Whitechapel, necessitated the concentration in particular localities of large bodies of police, and such an increase of force in one quarter of the Metropolis, it must be remembered, is only procurable by diminishing the number of men ordinarily employed in other divisions'. He goes on to complain that because of the extra men in Whitechapel that the consequence was 'diminished numbers of police in other quarters, and so long as the available force is hardly sufficient, as it is just now, for the performance of the ordinary and every day duties of the Police, and an additional drain on its resources leads to a diminished protection against, and consequent increase of, crime'. In his view the police were 'overworked, and under such circumstances crime cannot be met or coped with in a satisfactory and efficient manner'. Finally, with reference to the Ripper specifically he reported his regret that 'in spite of most strenuous efforts on the part of the Police, the criminal has up till now remained undiscovered'."

"The last part was a lie, of course, since as you now know I had now been on the case for a couple months, and had identified the person who I suspected was the Ripper … and in turn he, and others, had been removed from the streets. Perhaps having read the notes you can appreciate that the murder of Kelly was different to the rest."

"Indeed, I can, Holmes. Kelly was far younger than the other victims at just twenty-five-years old. It was also the only murder indoors, and it took place over five weeks after the previous ones, with the mutilations being far in excess of anything seen thus far. However, I think that I can explain most of these anomalies ... you said it was raining hard all that night, and so most of the unfortunate community would not venture out in such conditions, especially if they did not have anywhere indoors to take a client. Kelly was younger, fitter, more adventurous than most, and had a room on which she owed rent to boot, and so she would have been out soliciting for trade that evening for certain. I would say that she picked up the Ripper more likely in Commercial Street at the junction with Thrawl Street, rather than Thrawl Street itself, given that the former is a major throughfare in Spitalfields, and we know that the Ripper never strayed far from the main roads. It would have been a huge advantage for him to learn that he would not have to murder her in the street, but that he could do so in the privacy of her room at leisure. That is why the mutilations were so much in excess of anything else seen earlier, with the body being sliced open as opposed to treated like an animal carcass. He also did not have to worry about being seen after the event, for he could have cleaned himself up, maybe even using some of the victim's clothes to wipe away the blood before disposing of them in the fireplace. By the time he left at 5.45 a.m., trains would be running again, so he could make his way to any station, and simply disappear into the crowds like any other workman."

"Bravo, Watson! I believe that is exactly what happened, but why were there no murders during the whole of October do you suppose?"

"I have no idea, Holmes. The only explanation I can think of is because it was not possible for some reason. Maybe having nearly been caught on the night of the double event scared him off until his urge became so great that he thought it worthwhile taking the risk again."

"A possibility, but let's discuss that later in the comfort of your home, Watson. For now though, we should make for Liverpool Street station."

"Why?"

"Because at this time of morning it is the only place that I know in the vicinity that we stand a chance of hailing a cab!"

Chapter Eleven

The Alpha ...

On the way to the station, we passed the Providence Row night shelter [78], a Roman Catholic institution, which provided accommodation for over two-hundred-and-fifty persons. A huge building, three-storeys tall it looked like a modern hospital, with separate entrances for the men and women residents. Holmes commented that this place was responsible for saving many a woman from vice, and with the promise of bread and cocoa each morning and night, and even a soup and meat dinner if a Sunday, it was the only safe place that many an unfortunate might know. No vagrants, tramps, or professional beggars were admitted. Guests were allowed to stay for up to six-weeks at a time, and although the accommodation was simple it was most certainly better than the alternatives on offer in the vicinity.

Artillery Lane soon brought us to an even larger Gothic affair that dominated the area. Although it was perhaps the busiest of the railway termini in London, due in no small measure to its cheap workman's trains, it certainly was not the best, being a dirty and dingy amalgamation of two stations – Liverpool Street and Bishopsgate.

"It might interest you to learn, Watson, that when the new train shed was built a decade or so ago the supervisor of works was a Mr. Sherlock. As you recorded, my brother Mycroft once observed that you 'do hear of Sherlock everywhere', and that phrase seems to be true, at least in this instance!"

"I didn't think you took any notice of my writings, Holmes ... are you sure that you're not a secret fan after all?

Holmes declined to respond.

As we turned the corner into Liverpool Street itself, there in front of the Great Eastern Hotel was a lone cab. It must have presented a comical sight to anybody who might have seen us at that time of day, as we both as one increased our pace from a stroll, to a brisk walk, and then to pedestrianism – that peculiar form of competitive walking – lest somebody else suddenly appeared from the hotel to engage the vehicle of our desire before we could reach it that cold morning. Of course, the street was devoid of life at that time, and so thankfully no one saw this bizarre spectacle. Within seconds we were on our way to my home in Queen Anne Street, Marylebone.

It was only then, ensconced in a corner of the cab, and beginning to warm up a little, that I remembered something from the Ripper File that I had meant to query earlier.

"Holmes," said I, "that letter written to the Home Secretary by Robert Anderson on the twenty-third of October mentioned five victims, but at the time of writing there had only been four murders. Did he make a mistake, or was there another event about which we know nothing?"

"How very observant of you, Watson. I was wondering if you would spot that anomaly. The unfortunate he was referring to is Martha Tabram who died in the August."

"So why did you not mention her until now?"

"Because, my dear Watson, she was not a victim of the Ripper. You seem to forget that in the normal course of events that murders continue with, or without, a Ripper figure. For the East End there might be half a dozen murders of such women in an average year. Normally, it is easy to determine the culprits who are either the client of the lady in question, or a gang member trying to rob the unfortunate of their night's earnings, or a purely domestic incident in which case the suspect is most likely the husband or partner of the victim. The Ripper murders are only of note since they took place within a few months of each other, and were accomplished by horrific mutilations, which made them unique."

"But surely Anderson must have had some cause to believe that this was a Ripper killing?"

"Pass me the book, Watson, and I will save you some time by giving you a brief summary of the murders both before and after those that we have already considered, and then hopefully you will agree with me that there were only five deaths that can be attributed to the Ripper, and not the thirteen that some propose."

I did as I was instructed, being taken aback by the thought that there might have been as many as thirteen poor souls murdered at the hands of the that fiend. Holmes turned the pages until he found the relevant starting place for the discourse that was to follow.

"I will come to Martha Tabram presently, but let us investigate the deaths chronologically, in which case the first, and least likely, is that of Annie Millwood at the end of February 1888. At the time of her death she was the thirty-eight-year-old widow of a soldier by the name of Richard Millwood living at Spitalfields Chambers, No. 8 White's Row **[79]** in Spitalfields within spitting distance of Mary Kelly's address. However, there is no evidence to suggest that she was a prostitute. Millwood was admitted to the Whitechapel Workhouse Infirmary with stab wounds to her legs and lower part of her abdomen on the 25th February. She claimed to have received the injuries from a man with a clasp knife, though some say that her story was a fabrication, and that the wounds were self-inflicted."

"Why on earth would she do that? It seems a little extreme if her intention was just to get admitted to the questionable comforts of the workhouse infirmary."

"I agree, Watson. She most likely received her injuries in a fight of some sort. In any event she was treated and made a good recovery over the coming weeks. On the twenty-first of March she was sent to the South Grove Workhouse where on the thirty-first of March she was seen to fall to the ground while engaged in 'some occupation' at the rear of the building. She was dead, and according to the subsequent inquest her earlier injuries played no part in her collapse. The cause of death stated by the coroner was a 'sudden effusion into the pericardium from the rupture of the left pulmonary artery through ulceration'. The jury, quite correctly, returned a verdict of death from natural causes."

"So where is the Ripper connection?" I queried.

"Simply that some of those who now view the Ripper as being responsible for every death in the East End at that time claim that he used Millwood to 'learn his trade', just as he might have done with the next proposed victim."

"I see what you mean, Holmes ... and just who is next?"

"Ada Wilson [80] of Maidman Street in Mile End on the twenty-eighth of March just after midnight. She was a seamstress, and also a prostitute, at least according to her neighbour, Rose Bierman, who said that she 'often had visitors to see her'. On the day in question, she answered a knock to her front door, and was confronted by a man who forced his way in, and demanded money before stabbing her twice in the throat. Neighbours nearly caught him as he fled. Wilson survived and was able to describe the attacker to the police. He was about thirty-years old, five-and-a-half-feet tall, had a sunburnt face with a fair moustache, and wore a dark coat, light trousers, and a hat with a low crown and a very wide brim."

"The assailant's tan would indicate to him having been abroad ... and in that area most likely a sailor I would say, and when combined with the hat in the style that might be worn by an American or Quaker, he could not have been that hard to find. The description certainly does not resemble any of those associated with the Ripper, and besides Mile End is too far from his usual hunting ground, Holmes."

"Your reasoning is quite sound, Watson. The mystery person was probably a former client, who therefore knew that Wilson would be alone and might have money about the house. It could also be supposed that she in turn would have recognised him as such. Indeed, there is only her word for it that the man was intent on robbery. It could equally have been an altercation that arose over something related to her gentleman callers. The fact that she said nothing further may have meant that she was trying to conceal something. Maybe she did not want to reveal that she was a prostitute, in which case she may have known and feared further reprisals from the attacker. Whatever the truth might be there is little reason for a seamstress to have callers after midnight, unless she was a prostitute and he a client."

Holmes paused briefly while he turned the page.

"Ah, we now proceed to April 1888 and the death of Emma Smith [81]. She was, like so many women in the area, an unfortunate and an alcoholic. Smith lived in Whitechapel, was forty-five-years old, and destitute. By all accounts she wandered the streets looking for clients. A police report authored by Detective Inspector Edmund Reid, who you will recall also worked on the Mary Jane Kelly murder, on the sixteenth of April has her as living at a lodging house at No. 18 George Street, Spitalfields. Just after midnight on the third of April she had been observed in Limehouse at the junction of Farrance Street and Burdett Road talking to a man, likely a prospective client, dressed in dark clothes with a white scarf."

"Is this to be another instance of the client being the murderer?" I enquired.

"Not this time, Watson, at least the police did not think that the man with the white scarf was in any way involved with what happened next. Approximately four hours later she informed Mary Russell, the deputy-keeper at her lodging house, that she had been assaulted and robbed, and that her 'private parts had been injured'. This attack, often referred to as the Osborn Street murder, actually took place, according to the police report, opposite No. 10 Brick Lane by the Taylor's cocoa factory close to where Brick Lane becomes Osborn Street. This is where just four months earlier a friend of hers, Margaret Hames, or Hayes in some references, had been beaten, but not fatally. Smith was taken to the London Hospital for examination, and died there at 9 a.m. on the fourth of April, with the police not being informed of the death for another two days. She had died from internal bleeding, which included a blunt object which had penetrated the peritoneum. She had used clothing from her shoulders and placed it between her legs to try and arrest the bleeding. There were also wounds to her head and ear."

"What a dreadful and sadistic way to die. Violent as it was the injures are not akin to anything like those the Ripper might have inflicted."

"Quite so, Watson. In this instance it is almost certain that Smith had been the victim of a small gang of youths. She had even said that one of her attackers was about nineteen-years old who had approached her with the intention of robbing her of any money she might have earned that evening. It can only be speculation, but maybe having found that she had little money about her person the gang then decided not to violate her in the usual appalling way but to maim her instead, causing the horrific internal injuries which led to the poor soul's death."

"I can certainly see your point, Holmes. The East End was certainly no place for any woman to be alone at night ... attacks and deaths were happening on a pretty regular basis even without the Ripper at large."

"And now I come to Martha Tabram [82] who was murdered in the same month as Polly Nichols and, as you will learn, was stabbed multiple times in a frenzied manner that could at first be mistaken for a Ripper killing, and no doubt this is why Anderson considered it just so. However, I believe that the murderer was somebody else ... somebody almost as repulsive as the Ripper, with an attempt by the authorities to conceal the culprit who was known to them from the beginning."

"Surely you are not suggesting corruption within the Metropolitan Police, Holmes?"

"Not exactly, but in another official force as I will now relate. Tabram was found at 4.50 a.m. on Tuesday the seventh of August on the first-floor landing of George Yard Buildings [83]. She was thirty-nine-years old, an alcoholic, and a known unfortunate. Her corpse was discovered lying in a pool of blood, on her back, her hands by her sides, her legs apart, and with her clothes turned up to leave her lower body and legs exposed. She had been there since at least since 3.30 a.m. when Alfred Crow, a cab driver returning home, had seen the body but he had assumed that it was just a vagrant sleeping rough.

However, she was not there before 2 a.m. when another resident passed the same spot and observed nothing."

"What did the police do?" I enquired, eager to know the full details.

"Yet again it was Detective Inspector Edmund Reid who took statements from residents, but none could provide any useful information to advance the enquiry. In fact, nobody interviewed recognised Tabram as being a resident in the building, which did not have a reputation of being used for prostitution. It was later revealed that she had, up until a few weeks before her death, been living at No. 4 Star Place in Commercial Road."

"A mystery then as to why she should be found there in the first place."

"Indeed. The doctor who attended and examined the corpse [84] found no fewer than thirty-nine stab wounds. Despite the obvious assumption from the body position that she had been engaged in sexual intercourse, Dr. Killeen found no evidence of this activity, though there was a great deal of blood between her legs. The post-mortem showed that among the stab wounds five were to the left lung, two to the right lung, five to the liver, two to the spleen, six to the stomach, and a fatal one to the heart. It appeared that two different weapons had been used, one akin to a common knife, even a pen knife, while the other would be more like a dagger or bayonet such as might be carried by a soldier."

"This doesn't sound like the Ripper at all for the murder weapon was not the same, neither were the mutilations in that no body parts were removed or missing, and the throat was not slit."

"My conclusion exactly, Watson. However, a suspect, or rather a whole regiment of suspects, was soon to come to light, since, at 2 a.m. on the day in question, Police Constable Thomas Barrett, while on his beat, reported speaking with a soldier in George Yard close to George Yard Buildings [85]. The soldier said that he was waiting for a mate who had 'gone away with a girl'. Barrett thought nothing of it at the time, but that soldier who was with the 'girl' was now the prime suspect. Barrett described the soldier he spoke to as being a Grenadier Guard, in his early to mid-twenties, of medium height, dark hair, with a small dark brown moustache turned up at the ends. He sported a good conduct badge, but was without any medals."

"He shouldn't have been that hard to find. Were not the Grenadiers barracked at the Tower of London at that time?"

"Correct again, Watson. Reid and Barrett went to the Tower to make enquiries on the same day, and on the following day a parade of all privates and corporals that were on leave at the time of the murder was held. Barrett identified a private who was wearing medals, but when asked to identify the soldier a second time he chose a different guardsman. It seems that Barrett may have identified the correct soldier first time, but was then swayed by the medals he was wearing, and so picked another soldier without medals the second time around."

"I would say it likely that the private that Barrett spoke to in George Yard was, in fact, the murderer on his way back to barracks who happened to come across the policeman, and thinking on his feet made up the story about waiting for his mate. He might well have worn medals, which he quickly hid in a pocket since he knew that they could easily be used to identify him later. Did not Reid work this out for himself and make an arrest, or at least question the soldier further?"

"Actually, he did not since the waters were to be muddied by another witness who came forward. 'Pearly' Poll, whose real name was Mary Connelly, stated that she and Tabram had been with two soldiers up until just before midnight. She was able to identify one of the men as being a corporal, but that was the soldier that she had accompanied to Angel Court. Another parade was held for Connelly three days later on the strength of this but she pronounced that the uniforms were wrong. The men she and Tabram had been with sported white bands around their caps ..."

"The sign of the Coldstream Guards," I interjected.

"Precisely, and they reside not at the Tower, but at Wellington Barracks near Buckingham Palace. A subsequent inspection of the soldiers at Wellington Barracks by Connelly proved unsatisfactory as, although she was able to positively identify two soldiers by the names of George and Skipper, both of them had solid alibis, and neither were corporals."

"So, who was the culprit, Holmes?"

"We will never know. The inevitable verdict of 'wilful murder by person or persons unknown' was returned. It seems clear to me that Reid was on the right track in suspecting the murderer to be a soldier, and might even have interviewed the killer, but was hindered in his investigation by his two witnesses. I cannot prove it, but I very much suspect that they might have been approached and made to give false testimony. After all it would not look good to have a member of Her Majesty's forces convicted of murdering an unfortunate in such a manner."

"Having been a serving officer myself, I know that soldiers will close ranks and do almost anything to save the honour of the regiment, and hence, reluctantly, I must agree with your hypothesis."

Holmes glanced out of the cab window.

"I observe that we are already in Theobalds Road, so I barely have time to tell you of the possible Ripper murders after that of Mary Kelly. Do you still wish me to proceed, or have you heard enough to convince you that there were only five such events attributable to the Ripper?"

"Oh, no, Holmes. This is fascinating, please do continue."

Chapter Twelve

... And Omega

Our cab passed Montague Street, where Holmes had lived prior to us both taking up residence in Baker Street, and then the magnificent Greek temple inspired columns, triangular pediment, and enormous steps of the British Museum came into view. A wonderous place full of objects with hidden secrets, but on this particular morning there was no time to reflect upon them for Holmes's account had my full attention.

"It was six weeks after the Mary Kelly murder, when life was returning to normal in the East End, and when the *non de plume* Jack the Ripper was fast fading from the public's lips that there came the death of Catherine Rose Mylett [86] just five days before Christmas. She went by a variety of names including 'Drunken Lizzie', and 'Fair Alice', and was most assuredly both an unfortunate and an alcoholic. At 2.30 a.m. on the twentieth of December she was spotted outside The George Tavern in Commercial Road in the company of two men, who might well have been the same two men she had been seen talking with six hours earlier in Poplar High Street. It was at 4.15 a.m. that Police Sergeant Robert Golding found her body in Clarke's Yard, a builder's merchant, between No. 184 and No. 186 Poplar High Street. The body was on its left side with the left leg drawn up, and the right leg stretched out. Some say this was reminiscent of a Ripper killing, albeit without any signs of injury."

I pointed out that it could equally have been an attempt by a good Samaritan to place the body of a drunken person who had passed out in the street on their side, so that they would not choke on their own vomit should they be sick. Holmes acknowledged my contribution with a nod, and then continued his narrative.

"It was only much later under the closer examination of Dr. Matthew Brownfield, who performed the post-mortem, that a faint mark, such as might be made by a cord being pulled tight around the neck from the spine to the left ear suggested strangulation. Blood was oozing from the nostrils, and there were impressions of the thumbs, middle, and index fingers of someone plainly visible on each side of the neck. Catherine had been attacked from behind, and had recently ingested food comprising of meat and potatoes. A search of the area was done by a Dr. Robert Anderson, but he reported that there was no sign of a struggle in that nothing had been strewn about, no clothing had been ripped or torn, there were no scratches on the body, and no second set of footprints to be seen on the soft ground in the yard. The conclusion was that the body 'lay naturally'."

"Could it have been that she was strangled elsewhere, and the body placed carefully in the yard afterwards?"

"Well not according to the police who chose to accept Anderson's natural causes version of events, since that required far less paperwork, and no possibility of a murder investigation."

"Sounds to me like another instance of a cover up as with Martha Tabram, Holmes."

"A thought that I also entertained, or at least the possibility that the force did not want to reveal another murder lest it reignite panic in the East End, or maybe because they had just become lazy. However, it wasn't to be the latter, since Anderson insisted upon another professional opinion, so our old friend Dr. Thomas Bond was summoned. You will remember that name from earlier as he was involved with the post-mortem of Catherine Eddowes."

"I recall that you did not think very highly of him."

"Quite correct, Watson. Perhaps fortuitously, the request for his services was intercepted by Bond's assistant who, along with the Senior Police Surgeon, went to examine the body for themselves. They both agreed on the original diagnosis of strangulation."

"I wager that Bond was not best pleased at being sidelined in that fashion, Holmes."

"He was not, and later when Bond did examine the corpse, he found no trace of strangulation as the faint marks had by now disappeared. As you know yourself, Watson, normally there would be additional secondary signs of strangulation, such as a protruding tongue or clenched fists, but these, too, were missing. Bond put forward the unlikely theory that she had merely collapsed due to drink, and choked to death by her stiff velvet collar."

"As unlikely a theory as I ever did hear, Holmes, but what did the inquest say?"

"That was presided over by Wynne Baxter who wanted nothing to do with this 'nonsense' of death caused by 'natural causes'. He pointed out that Bond did not see the body until five days after the death, and so his observations could not be given too much credence. The verdict of 'wilful murder by persons or persons unknown' was forthcoming, but despite this the police refused to take any further action, deeming it to be a waste of their resources."

"An unhappy day for justice, but hardly a Ripper killing as the method was all wrong, and Poplar is hardly close to where any of the other victims met their deaths."

"Our next victim though, Alice McKenzie [87], or 'Clay Pipe' Alice as she was commonly known, met her end right in the middle of what might be termed 'Ripperland'. She had been living in a lodging house in Gun Street since April 1888, and working for some Jewish neighbours as a washerwoman and charwoman, and to supplement her income was also a prostitute, and fond of both drink and tobacco ... preferably in a pipe."

"And hence her nickname," I interjected just to prove that even at this early hour I was still following what Holmes was relating. He nodded in appreciation of my comment.

"On the sixteenth of July 1889 her partner, John McCormack, returned home from work at approximately 4 p.m., and gave McKenzie 1s. 8d. to pay the rent plus a further 1s. for household expenses. She never did pay the rent, but instead went with a blind boy called George Dixon, who was also a resident at the lodging, to the Royal Cambridge Music Hall. Afterwards she returned home, and then left again around 8.30 p.m. following an argument with McCormack. She was observed leaving by Elizabeth Ryder, the manager of the lodging house, who stated that she was drunk at the time. This contradicted the account given by McCormack who said that he did not see McKenzie after 4 p.m. that day."

"I can tell already that McCormack is going to be the culprit with the motive being that McKenzie had spent all the rent and housekeeping money for the week which sent him into a rage."

"Not so fast, old friend. You should never jump to a conclusion before you have heard all the evidence. Later that evening, just before midnight, McKenzie was spotted in the vicinity of Flower and Dean Street and Brick Lane. At 12.45 a.m. it began to rain, and five minutes later Police Constable Walter Andrews, on his beat, entered Castle Alley, which is just off Whitechapel High Street. Close to a lamp post he discovered McKenzie's body [88] with two stab wounds to the left side of her neck. Her skirt had been lifted, and her abdomen mutilated. The body was not there at 12.20 a.m. when Andrews had last passed the spot. A resident in Castle Alley who was reading in bed at the time reported hearing nothing unusual until he heard Andrews blowing his whistle to summon assistance."

"It could be that McCormack followed her to that spot and then murdered her, but equally I think that having spent the weekly income she felt somewhat guilty, and was endeavouring to earn some money on the street, and simply got into a confrontation with a client."

Holmes cleared his throat, and coughed in such a manner that it told me that I should refrain from interrupting with such speculative comments.

"The two men called upon to investigate will be familiar to you by now ... Detective Inspector Reid and Dr. Phillips were both at the scene shortly after 1.00 a.m. The pavement beneath the body was dry, placing the time of death before 12.45 a.m. when the rain had started. Further examination of the corpse [89] revealed that the cause of death was the severing of the carotid artery. In addition, there were two stab wounds to the neck, bruising on the chest, five bruises on the abdomen, a long cut between the left breast and navel, multiple scratches from the navel toward the genitalia, and a small cut across the *mons veneris*. Although, at first, it might look like a Ripper killing, there were differences in that the wounds were much shallower, the implement used much smaller, and it was all done by a left-handed person. However, somebody else was about to stir things up a little."

"Not Bond again?" said I, almost as a reflex reaction.

"Indeed, it was, Watson. Whereas Phillips maintained that it was not consistent with being the work of the Ripper, Bond, who would examine the body the day after the post mortem, was convinced that it was just such a killing."

"And with whom did the police side with this time, Holmes?"

"They were not of one mind either ... Police Commissioner James Monro, who had been present at the murder scene at 3 a.m., was inclined to believe that the Ripper had returned, whereas Assistant Police Commissioner Robert Anderson, who had been on holiday at the time of the murder on his return, pronounced that it was not. For some weeks an extra twenty-two officers were put on duty to reassure the public. The inquest returned a verdict of 'murder by a person or persons unknown'."

"And your view, Holmes."

"I believe that you are right in that it was an altercation with a client, but not the Ripper on account of the wounds being so shallow."

"It seems to me that with each of these other cases that the Ripper is exonerated mainly on account of the lack of injuries."

"That may be, but the body found at 5.20 a.m. on the tenth of September 1889 by Police Constable William Pennett under a railway arch at Pinchin Street will go against that assertion, Watson [90]."

"Was it badly disfigured then, Holmes?"

"You could say that ... it was a headless torso," said he with a thin smile upon his lips.

"Was an identification ever made?"

"No. There was extensive bruising to the back, hip and arm, indicating that the female victim, whom it was estimated was between thirty and forty-years of age, had been severely beaten prior to death. The abdomen was mutilated, but the genitalia were not touched. No other body parts were found in the area, and it was assumed from this, and the lack of blood, that the victim was murdered elsewhere, and subsequently dumped in Pinchin Street."

"You mentioned a railway arch, so was she thrown from a passing train above?"

"If it weren't for the fact that she was so far under the arch it would have been a reasonable hypothesis, albeit there were few trains at that time of day. The corpse was not there twenty minutes earlier when Pennett had last passed the same spot on his beat. A closer inspection revealed that there was blood inside the torso, a sign that death was not from the cutting of the throat. It was also determined that the victim was killed between twenty-four and thirty-six hours prior to the finding of the body. The killing was certainly a gruesome one, and in the right location to be the work of the Ripper. However, given that the mutilations did not match the type of injuries inflicted upon other Ripper victims, and that they might have been performed anywhere in London, it is unlikely that this murder can be attributed to him, despite the speculation of some newspaper reports at the time. As Chief Commissioner Monro put it, 'there was no sign of frenzied mutilation of the body, but of deliberate and skilful dismemberment with a view to removal of the limbs'."

"Were there no clues to enable further enquiries to be made?"

"It is quite probable that this murder was connected with a series of similar killings that Scotland Yard were already investigating. In fact, this was remarked upon by Assistant Chief Constable Macnaghten who wrote that 'the stomach was split up by a cut, and the head and legs had been severed in a manner identical with that of a woman whose remains were discovered in the Thames, in Battersea Park, and along the Chelsea Embankment on the fourth of June of the same year; and these murders had no connection whatever with the Whitechapel horrors. The Rainham mystery in 1887, and the Whitehall mystery in 1888 were of a similar type to the Thames and Pinchin Street crimes'. The bodies became known as the Thames Torso murders case that included at least four deaths which were never solved. Only one body was ever identified … a homeless prostitute from Chelsea called Elizabeth Jackson."

"Sounds like there was another Ripper on the loose, only one attacking unfortunates in the West End."

"The manner of those killings was less Ripper-like and struck me as being more likely to be motivated by revenge, Watson … revenge by somebody who had a control over those women, and used their deaths to strike terror in others lest they should end up the same way."

"I suspect we will never know, Holmes. However, if my mathematics is correct there is but one victim left to consider?"

"Correct on both counts, literally, Watson. The final possible Ripper murder was that of Frances Coles **[91]**. Her body was found under a railway arch at Swallow Gardens on Friday the thirteenth of November 1891 by Police Constable Ernest Thompson. It was, in fact, little more than an alleyway running under the railway line, and not far from where the Pinchin Street torso was discovered. It was 2.15 a.m. and Thompson was quite sure that the body was not there when he had passed the same spot on his beat fifteen minutes earlier. He reported having heard footsteps during his approach, so he might well have interrupted the murderer but, following correct police procedure, he stayed with the body and did not attempt to investigate the sound. On examination he observed that Coles was lying in a pool of blood with her throat cut from ear to ear. He called for assistance by blowing his whistle, and very soon he had been joined by Police Constables Hyde, Hinton, and Elliott, the latter having been on plain-clothes duty in nearby Royal Mint Street."

"On first inspection it does sound like the beginning of a Ripper mutilation, albeit a year after the last murder," said I, trying to make some connection between the two.

"Unbelievably, it was discovered that that there was still a faint pulse, though by the time Dr. Frederick Oxley arrived, Coles was dead. Meanwhile Police Constable Hinton had gone to get a senior police officer who on arrival ordered that the crime scene be left untouched, while officers were directed to search the area and question anybody on the streets at the time. Our old friend, Dr. Bagster Phillips was soon at the scene and stated that although horrific, the lack of mutilation was not consistent with it being the work of the Ripper. The body [92] was identified the following day as being Frances Coles, or Cole in some reports, a prostitute who at one time had worked in the Minories as a labeller of bottles at a wholesale chemists, and had until recently lodged in Thrawl Street, until she had been forced to leave due to rent arrears."

"So, yet another poor unfortunate on the streets meets their end at the hands of a client I suppose?"

"Maybe, Watson. Just a few hours before her murder she had returned to Thrawl Street and asked her former landlady, Mrs. Hague, to allow her to return if she were able to clear her debts. On questioning, the landlady said that she had later seen Coles in a public house in Montague Street with a man of fair complexion, and sporting a moustache. It did not take the police long to find the man in question, James Sadler, and from his statement to the police the last couple of days of Coles's life became clearer."

"Alternatively, I suspect this Sadler person."

"You are guessing before any evidence has been presented, Watson, a deplorable habit which I hoped was confined only to those in the official forces. Sadler was a fifty-three-year old merchant seaman and fireman on the *Fez*, and had known Coles, in the capacity of a client, since the February. Two days prior to the murder they had visited The Princess Alice public house, and then spent the night together at Spitalfields Chambers, a common lodging house. They were still together the following day, and seemed to go on a tour of various East End hostelries for most of it. That evening, a drunk Coles purchased a black crepe hat from a milliners at No. 25 Nottingham Street, paying for her purchase with 2s. 6d. which Sadler had given her. Sadler was still with her, though he did not enter the shop. Later that evening while walking together in Thrawl Street, Sadler was attacked and robbed of his watch and money by two men and a woman in a red shawl. It was after this that they went their separate ways, since Sadler was angry that Coles did not come to his assistance. It was even suggested that Coles might have instigated the attack in the first place.

"It wasn't Sadler's day, was it?"

"However, they met again at the lodging house where they had spent the previous night, but now, having no money to pay for the accommodation they both had to leave. Sadler left first having been cleaned up by the night watchman following the attack. Coles left later, sometime after midnight, once she had come around from passing out from drink in the kitchen."

"Not entirely unexpected," said I.

"At around 1.45 a.m. she was in the company of another prostitute, Ellen Callana, in Commercial Street, and was solicited by 'a violent man in a cheese cutter hat'. Whereas Callana refused the client and received a black eye from him, Frances did not and went off with him in the direction of Minories."

"And what about Sadler?"

"He had headed back to his ship, but became involved in a fight with a group of dockworkers ... as you said Watson, it just wasn't his night! He was next seen on the pavement outside the Royal Mint by a police officer on his beat. He was described as being 'drunk and bloodied'. He was probably in no fit state to commit a murder, though he was certainly in the vicinity at the time Coles was murdered, but then so was 'Mr. Cheese Cutter Hat'."

"Do not berate me, Holmes, but I am guessing that the police arrested Sadler instead of looking for this other person. Am I right?"

"Correct, Sadler was subsequently questioned at Leman Street police station for around forty hours, following which he was formally charged with the murder. Potentially damning evidence came to light a few hours after the murder. Sadler had sold his knife to one Donald Campbell, possibly to get rid of it. Campbell had subsequently sold it on to a marine stores dealer."

"That does seem to be a rather black mark against him, Holmes."

"On the contrary, Watson. It tells me that he was innocent, for if he wanted to dispose of that piece of most damaging evidence, and being only a street or so away from the largest rubbish bin in London, why did he not simply divest himself of the knife by throwing it in the river? At the inquest it appeared very likely that Sadler would be found guilty, until it was revealed that his knife was so blunt that it would have been unable to cut a throat in the manner observed. As to the assertion that he was the Ripper, this was easy to rebut since Sadler could prove that he was at sea when some of the murders took place. Eventually in the March good sense prevailed and it was announced that 'no further evidence should now be offered against the accused'."

"Justice was done then."

"Yes, but it was a close-run thing, Watson. As he left the court a free man, he was cheered by a large crowd who had been convinced of his innocence all along. It seems clear that it was 'Mr. Cheese Cutter Hat' that the police should have concentrated on finding, though many at Scotland Yard were still of the opinion that Sadler was guilty. Sadler was extremely lucky in that he had proper legal representation in court paid for by the Seaman's Union. The outcome might well have been very different if he had not, so never forget that the quality of justice is a commodity that may be purchased."

"Sadly, I can only agree with you, Holmes, and having listened to all the evidence that you have presented, I am bound to accept your conclusion that there were only the five Ripper murders."

At that our cab slowed as the driver had reached Queen Anne Street and was now straining his eyes in the early pre-dawn light searching for the property number that I had given him at Liverpool Street. I intervened and directed him to my house, and once outside paid him the fare along with a generous tip, which was gratefully received with a doff of his cap. On the raised step by my front door, I whispered to Holmes so as not to wake the household who would hopefully still be asleep for a few hours to come.

"You are fortunate in that my writings upon our adventures, although of little merit in your estimation, do strike some accord with the general public, and have provided me with enough income so that I can offer you a bed upon which to rest, rather than the sitting room sofa. At the top of the stairs if you turn right, the second door on the left will reveal an empty bedroom. You are welcome to it for as long as you wish. First thing I will send somebody around to Baker Street to collect our respective luggage from Mrs. Hudson."

"Excellent, Watson, but if it is all the same to you, I would prefer first to avail myself of your sitting room in which I feel certain I will discover a decanter of brandy. I will also help myself to a cigar or two before I retire. Conversely, you should make straight for your bedroom as I deduce that your wife will have missed you greatly these past days."

"Very well. I suggest that both of us will rise too late for breakfast, so let us reconvene at lunchtime when the true identity of the Ripper may be revealed."

With that I carefully opened the front door, and made off up the stairs, while Holmes went in the direction of the sitting room, where the two forms of poison he sought awaited him in both quantity and quality.

Chapter Thirteen

Denouement

It was nearly an hour past midday when Holmes finally joined me in the sitting room. He had clearly needed the rest following his journey up from Sussex the previous day, and subsequent investigations in the East End, which had extended until near dawn. In fact, I could tell immediately that those usually razor-sharp deductions of his had yet to awaken along with the rest of his physical being. He helped himself to some tea from the tray that the housekeeper placed on the side table, and sat down in a leather armchair, not unlike his preferred seat in our old Baker Street rooms, and stared out of the window into the narrow road, which at all times was relatively quiet since this was a residential area unlike that of our former shared abode.

"I trust you had a good sleep as well, Watson, and are now ready to make your deductions to support whatever you have written down in your sealed letter from yesterday?"

From his pocket he produced both his envelope and mine, and placed them upon the table next to the teapot.

"Are there any amendments that you wish to make first?"

"None at all, Holmes. All I learnt yesterday does nothing to damage my initial hypothesis. In fact, it only goes to strengthen the assertions that I have made."

"You are confident, my friend. Please begin your analysis," said he, in a commanding tone with just a slight hint of curiosity, or perhaps I also detected some frustration that nothing he had shown me the past eighteen hours had altered my original convictions.

"The first, and most certain, of my statements is that your final deduction as we entered this house earlier today was incorrect."

Holmes genuinely seemed shocked. He looked at me, then about the room, before fixing those piercing eyes of his on the untidy sofa. His expression changed to one of regret.

"I am most sorry, Watson. It was an assumption that I made upon the basis of how I would have responded. As you are aware I have never fully understood the female mind to the point of being able to predict an outcome with one-hundred percent success. It is like flipping a coin in that if five heads come up in succession, you would naturally bet that the next toss would result in a tail, but actually the chances are still only fifty percent ... just as they are always only fifty percent. I perceive then that after I retired that you came downstairs again and slept here. Your wife was not pleased at your return so early in the morning?"

"That would be a fair comment," said I, with some sarcasm. "She was not best pleased at all. In the first instance she had expected me to be away for several days with you in Sussex, not for us to travel to London together the following day, or for me to tire you out with late-night visits to the vilest part of the metropolis, only to return here to disturb her sleep in the small hours of the morning. She blames me for everything."

"I will gladly take full responsibility, Watson, as I would wish there to be no disharmony in your home on my part."

"Little chance of that, Holmes, for she left over an hour ago, and has gone to stay with her sister in Bedfordshire until further notice."

"She will eventually return, and when she does you might even have increased funds with which to buy her those new shoes that she has been wanting for months ... after all, you seem confident that you have the drop on me regarding the identity of the Ripper."

"I do ... but what shoes?"

"Quite frankly, I have no idea, but women will inevitably have some pair of shoes on their mind. Shoes which they will tell you that they have been wanting for months. You just have to find out which ones."

"Thank you, Holmes. That's a great help!"

"I am glad to be of service. Now what about the Ripper?"

"I believe that there is nothing to be deduced from the fact that all the women murdered were unfortunates. That was not the motive for the Ripper, and so it was not his desire to rid the East End of these unfortunate women. I think that it was more about opportunity, since at that time of night the only persons to be about on the streets would be such vulnerable women."

"Anything else?"

"Yes. He was like a fisherman casting his net among the five thousand souls in that part of London. What he caught in his net was therefore completely random."

"Very sound."

"The fact that all the victims, and by the way I have already agreed with you that there were only the five, were chronic alcoholics is also of no importance, since almost all unfortunates living in the East End were heavy drinkers. Though, it would certainly have helped the Ripper's cause since a drunken individual is easier to overpower, and has dulled reflexes and so would not have been aware of his intentions until it was too late to react."

"Do not forget, Watson, that the public houses acted as a shop window for many, especially if it were raining such as it was on several of the nights in question. Hence the Ripper may have met his victim inside such an establishment earlier in the evening, or he may have waited outside patiently for his victim to emerge and then followed them."

"Ah, but there is a flaw there, Holmes. If the Ripper had been inside, he would have been surrounded by other folk, and surely at least one of them would have come forward at the time with some sort of a description or suspicion."

"A very valid point, Watson. It is most likely then that the Ripper simply found his victims looking for clients on the streets, and had no need to keep watch on such places for the fish in this particular sea were plentiful."

"I did note that in each of the descriptions of the victims that hats and flowers were prominent. Polly Nichols was wearing a new straw bonnet, Annie Chapman used to sell flowers, Elizabeth Stride was wearing a red rose posy, Catherine Eddowes wore a skirt with a pattern of Michaelmas daisies and lilies and so on. Even Mary Jane Kelly was last heard singing *Only a Violet I Plucked from Mother's Grave* according to your file."

"And what of it, Watson? Are you implying that our perpetrator and harbinger of death was a mad florist?"

"No, Holmes. I am only suggesting that either the flowers or the sight of a new bonnet might have acted as an initial attraction for the Ripper."

"Maybe, but on the whole I think not. Remember that all but the last, Mary Kelly, was middle-aged and to put it bluntly ... not beauties. The Ripper took what was on offer regardless of looks. He might have considered himself lucky with Mary Kelly as she was younger, attractive, and had a place of her own in which to entertain. Remember that it had been raining hard most of that evening. Surely most women, even if they had the stamina, would not wish to be out in such conditions searching for clients if they had the 4d. required for a lodging."

"I also wondered if there could be anything in the name of Kelly? Catherine Eddowes also called herself Catherine Kelly after her current partner, and it does seem suspicious that the killings stopped after the death of Mary Kelly?"

"And just how do you suppose that the Ripper might know the names of his victims in advance, if, as you rightly say, they were selected at random?"

"Then there is that trinity of clues ... the Goulston Street graffito, the shouting of Lipski just prior to the Elizabeth Stride murder, and the 'Dear Boss' and other letters. Having considered all the evidence carefully I can only come to the same conclusion as you in that all are red herrings of one sort or another."

"Depressing, isn't it? Every lead thus far actually amounts to nothing."

"On the question of expertise though, I feel that we are on firmer ground. As you correctly pointed out, given that the conditions were not ideal under which to extract organs, the Ripper must have had some anatomical knowledge at least akin to that of a butcher or slaughterman. The killings were, as you have demonstrated, mostly conducted outdoors in wet conditions, in the cold, in the dark, and most probably with a single six-inch non-surgical long-bladed knife, so it is a miracle that anything was removed at all … cleanly or otherwise."

"And what about the fact that the Ripper coveted such organs?"

"It not only gave him trophies, Holmes, along with a sense of ownership, but also the ability to physically re-enact the killings in his mind at any time … perhaps even obtaining a sexual thrill. It is more usual to keep a piece of clothing or jewellery, but in sadistic and extreme cases such as this it is not so strange. It may have, in addition, given him a positive feeling of accomplishment."

I paused as I had run out of ideas for the present, and needed a few moments to collect my thoughts.

"Have I forgotten anything thus far, Holmes?"

"You have missed nothing, but at the same time you have only gone over old ground and produced little of interest. You are thinking like the official forces. Rather than concentrating on what the Ripper is not, why not make some deductions about what we do know to be true about him? Let me help you, as I believe it really is quite elementary, to use a word you are over-fond of using in your writings about our adventures."

"Do enlighten me then, Holmes," said I, somewhat piqued by his summary of my efforts thus far.

"Two important facts we have already established are that the Ripper worked alone and on foot. He had no access to any private form of transport. There were various descriptions of him given to the police, and one or more may have been correct, but in the main the descriptions seemed to contradict each other such that every foreigner, Jew, 'Leather Apron' and so on was a suspect. Clearly, the Ripper had a way of disappearing after each murder despite the increased police presence in the area. With the number of police officers and frequency of beat patrols raised to every fifteen minutes or so, it seems incredible that nobody ever saw the Ripper fleeing after the event, even though the police were often on the scene within minutes of an incident."

"The speculation was that the Ripper either had transport, such as a private carriage, or lived in the area. It is inconceivable that a horse drawn carriage, which immediately implies an accomplice, traversing the near empty streets of Whitechapel at such a time would not have been heard, seen, or attract any attention, especially when the Whitechapel Division of the Metropolitan Police had well over five hundred officers at their disposal in 1888. I feel sure that he did not live in the area, since despite the crime and poverty here the community is strong and supportive and would have voiced their suspicions immediately if one of their own were committing such atrocities."

"The police also carried out house-to-house searches, and made extensive enquiries at the common lodging houses, all to no avail. If the Ripper lived in Whitechapel, it would be expected that he would know the area intimately. The killings of the five victims all took place very close to the three main arteries running through the East End: Whitechapel Road, and its extension into Whitechapel High Street and Aldgate High Street, Commercial Road, and Commercial Street. Hence, it can be concluded that he did not know Whitechapel that well since he did not venture far from the main roads and kept away from the filthy courts and alleyways."

"Maybe he only knew of the area since he passed through it on his way to and from work."

"At last, you are getting somewhere, Watson. Of course, he was a working man as can be inferred by reference to the dates of the murders, all of which took place at weekends, or around public holidays. Polly Nichols was murdered on the Friday of a Bank Holiday weekend, Annie Chapman a Saturday, the night of the double event was a Sunday, and Mary Kelly was killed on a Friday."

"Wait a minute, Holmes, the Friday upon which Kelly was murdered was not a holiday, so your reasoning fails."

"No, it doesn't, Watson. In fact, it is the biggest clue of all for that Friday was the day of the Lord Mayor's Show, remember? And for workers in the City of London, especially those who work for the City of London Corporation itself, it is a public holiday to enable them to witness the grandest of processions as the new Lord Mayor journeys through the streets to swear his loyalty to the Crown."

"The Ripper then, not only lived outside of Whitechapel, but worked in the City of London, possibly for the Corporation itself, and for this reason was limited in his options as to when he could commit his terrible crimes."

"Exactly, Watson. The logical conclusion being that his hours of employment included either late nights or early mornings. Now let us return to the lack of a blood trail, which I believe is so important."

"You demonstrated very well that it would have been possible for him to escape via the railway lines, often goods yards, which at that hour would be deserted, except maybe for the odd workman attending to the tracks, and they could be easily avoided."

"There probably was a trail of blood to follow, but the police were looking in the wrong place. It may also have been that the Ripper changed shoes and clothes after each murder, in which case he would have need to carry some sort of a bag with him. And what would have been more natural than somebody dressed as a night worker carrying a tool bag? Taking it to its natural conclusion, the Ripper dressed as a member of a night time railway gang [93] simply because he was, or had been, a railway worker at some point, and so knew the railway lines of the East End better than the roads."

"If he was such a person that might also explain why the killing spree stopped so suddenly, Holmes."

"Do expand upon that statement, Watson."

"Working on the railway tracks was a hazardous job with many deaths and injuries each year. Most accidents were caused by human error due to tiredness, and this is not surprising. I read an article recently which said that the enginemen and firemen would commonly work between ten and eighteen hours a day, occasionally on a Sunday as well, and only receive two or three days of holiday a year. Other staff had long hours, too, with no railway employee working less than ten hours a day."

"Bravo, Watson. I had considered this myself and looked up the official accident reports for 1888 … there were at total of seventy-six incidents. For example, on the first of December that year a train was derailed due to excessive speed at Liverpool Street station, while on New Year's Eve nineteen people were injured at Norwood Junction in fog, and on the same day fifty-one were injured due to insufficient brakes at Loughborough Junction when a train overran a red signal. However, none of those accidents resulted in fatalities, but even more dangerous than being a passenger on a train, was to be a permanent way worker on the tracks with accidents and deaths going largely unrecorded. Hence, it is possible that the activities of the Ripper were curtailed by one of the frequent railway accidents of the time, though I doubt it."

"The railways certainly seem to figure prominently in this case," I reflected.

"There is even a further possibility in that they provide a reason why the attacks did not start earlier than the autumn of 1888. I checked, and the line out of Fenchurch Street to Tilbury opened a new route from Barking to Pitsea on the first of June that year with new stations serving West Horndon and Laindon. It is just conceivable that the Ripper lived close to one of those, and became a commuter into the City each day, which somehow became the trigger for his reign of terror. However, it is not likely since the summer of 1888 had been so wet that a landslip had occurred with that section of the line being partially closing until the winter. The only other candidate would be Gospel Oak station, which opened on the fourth of June 1888, with trains into Broad Street and Moorgate."

"So, in summary, Holmes, the Ripper was a loner from outside the Whitechapel area who worked in the City of London, possibly with a railway connection, who lived within commuting distance of central London, maybe in West Horndon, Laindon or Gospel Oak areas, who was to die, or be incapacitated, likely in a railway accident in late 1888. In any event he dressed in workman's clothes, carried a tool bag and, using his knowledge of the railways, was able to use goods yards or open stations to escape the scene of crime undetected."

"You have put it most succinctly, Watson. However, there are still two points to satisfy. First how did the Ripper acquire his anatomical knowledge, and second where was he heading on the night of the double event after the first killing? Answer those and you will have solved the case I believe."

"To address the second question first, Holmes, he was returning to the safety of his home."

"Or his place of work, given that if he did live outside of London there would have been no trains for some hours."

"Where do you believe he worked, Holmes?"

"Isn't it obvious? Again, ask yourself where he was going on the night of the double event. The Ripper wasn't just walking aimlessly around the streets, and writing up messages in chalk to confuse the police … if indeed that is what he did. Remember he had nearly been caught, and wanted to escape as quickly as possible, and for that he needed to gain access to the Underground tracks at Aldgate."

"I think I am beginning to understand your train of thought, if you will forgive the pun, Holmes? He was heading toward, not away from, the City of London itself, in which case if he continued his journey westward, depending on whether he took the north or south section of the Metropolitan railway, he would end up at either Mark Lane or Bishopsgate."

"Correct again, Watson. Mark Lane would at first glance seem ideal since it is only four-fifths of a mile from Aldgate and is the closest station to Billingsgate market."

"And that is where Joseph Barnett worked. That's it then … it was Barnett all along," said I with some excitement.

"He was certainly a suspect that I couldn't entirely eliminate. He would have had the skill necessary, and I need not remind you that Billingsgate is run by the City of London Corporation, and so would have been closed on all the days of the murders. A fish porter with blood on him would not have attracted any attention in that area normally but it is not to be."

"Why?"

"Because even if Barnett was our man, there is no way he could exit Mark Lane station, I assure you. It is very much a closed station with no opportunity to enter or exit after normal operating hours. There is also no reason to think that he had any in depth knowledge of the workings of the railways."

I looked crestfallen.

"You were along the right tracks though, even if in the wrong direction," said he, returning my pun with a broad smile upon his face.

"Bishopsgate, then?"

"A little further, Watson. One-and-a-third rail miles from Aldgate to be precise."

"Moorgate, or Aldersgate, but both of those are not what you would call open stations either."

"Indeed, but just after Farringdon, and prior to Aldersgate, on our Underground journey last night, did you not yourself remark upon some sidings [94]? If you recall I said at the time that it would be instructive to your investigation if you noted the route we took to Whitechapel."

It was only then that my brain finally registered Holmes's solution to the puzzle.

"The sidings that serve the Smithfield meat markets ... so that is where he got his anatomical knowledge!" I exclaimed.

"Yes, the entry to London's main meat market would have been simplicity itself for the Ripper, since that series of sidings from the main line run directly beneath Smithfield Park, and are used for the transfer of animal carcasses to its cold store with direct access to the markets above via lifts. Hence the Ripper could have reached his workplace without ever having to be seen on the streets of London, or arousing the least of suspicions. Furthermore, the markets are controlled by the City of London Corporation. They cover ten acres, and open around 2.00 a.m. so that, even if there was trading the Ripper with blood about his person would just fade into the background in that vast complex [95]."

"No doubt he would have been able to simply put his white market smock over his railway workmen's clothes, and should there be blood present nobody would be the wiser from where it came."

At that moment, Holmes smiled at the sight of a cab pulling up outside, and a corpulent man struggling with our bags, just collected from Baker Street, getting out and making his way, as best he could, to the front door. The bell rang and, as the housemaid was dispatched to answer it, Holmes continued.

"Do you remember by chance what Dickens said about Smithfield in *Oliver Twist*, which although a little dated now still gives a general impression of the area?"

"Actually, I believe, I do ... he said it was a place for 'the unwashed, unshaven, squalid and dirty figures constantly running to and fro' with the ground being 'covered, nearly ankle-deep, with filth and mire; a thick steam perpetually rising from the reeking bodies of the cattle'."

"Equally as squalid as anything to be found in Whitechapel, and no doubt an area where cheap accommodation could be had, and also a place where somebody, such as the Ripper, could reside undetected for some months."

"Months, Holmes?"

"Yes, there is one final piece to this jigsaw puzzle which might be of importance, for I discovered that it was only in the summer of 1888 that the so-called Annexe Market building came into being. Hence it is possible that the Ripper only moved into the area when he found work in that particular part of the market, and that it in some way affected him, and acted as the catalyst for what was to follow in the autumn."

"And you identified such a person for the police?"

"Alas, no, Watson. I merely informed Mycroft of my theory, and he in turn told the Chief Commissioner that they should be looking for somebody who had only worked in the markets for a few months, lived in the Smithfield area, and who had previously worked on the railways. The police then did what they do best, and a couple of weeks later at the end of November I received a letter of thanks along with information that several persons had been removed from the streets, and detained in institutions indefinitely."

"Are you not ashamed, or at least a little disturbed, that since it is agreed that the Ripper worked alone, and that more than one individual was put away without trial, that all but one of those arrested was, in fact, innocent?"

"It does weigh on my mind sometimes, Watson, but they were desperate times, and I do believe that my solution was the right one, even though I have no name for the individual concerned. Anyway, those are the details I wrote down inside my sealed envelope. Perhaps you would care examine the contents now?"

I did, and they were exactly as Holmes had just related to me. It was hard to be angry with the man for long, for he, too, had been placed in an impossible position in that he was only brought in after several murders had already taken place, and then only in a consultancy role with no real powers afforded to him. He had done his best, and had come up with a unique solution overlooked by others. A solution I might add that can neither be proved nor disproved, though with the absence of any further murders I am inclined to think that Holmes was correct in his analysis.

"And what of your theory, Watson? I would be interested to know what you wrote, and whether I am to enjoy dinner at Simpson's this evening at your expense?"

I waved my hand in a motion that signified that he could open my envelope. He did so, and at first, he looked quite astonished, then he cackled so heartily that I thought he might do himself some injury.

"It's impossible, Watson," said he. "It is the very same conclusion that I came to, only with a couple of embellishments of your own."

"I hope you brought your cheque book with you, Holmes?" said I, in jest.

He rose, and paced the room in silence for a minute or two.

"I know when I am defeated, Watson ... but not by you as there is another power at work here, isn't there? It is a conspiracy I tell you, but the kindest conspiracy I ever did witness, and don't think that I didn't notice who it was that arrived with our bags moments ago ... you can tell my brother to come in now."

The housekeeper opened the door right on cue, and there stood a beaming Mycroft Holmes.

"Brother Sherlock, we were both worried about you."

"Why?"

"Because since you moved from London, your two best friends in the world have heard nothing from you since, Sherlock."

"I have been busy with my bees ... there really was no need to brood so, Mycroft. I am flattered, though, that you should collaborate with Watson in such a way, and devise this subterfuge to get me back here, and working again."

"I knew that if Watson came to see you with such a challenge that you could not resist. Naturally the cards were stacked in his favour, as I had already taken the precaution to brief him fully about your Ripper File, and the findings therein, of which you had appraised me at the time."

"We really were both most concerned as to your health," said I. "In addition, I truly wanted to find out more about those horrific events back in 1888, and to learn if justice was ever done for those poor unfortunate souls that suffered at the hands of Jack the Ripper."

"I must admit that I have been somewhat depressed of late without even knowing it, and seeing you both again is the tonic I needed. I am only sorry that within this charade I caused Mrs. Watson some anguish."

"Actually, Holmes, you didn't. It was all part of our joint strategy. You were not to know that although we have this adequately sized property, my wife and I have no servants. It was, in fact, her contribution in that although we have been married since 1902, she has never met you and so it was easy for her to pretend to be the housemaid and open the door just now, and to also serve the tea earlier. I merely told you of our supposed argument, and ruffled the cushions on the sofa a little, to see if I could fool you. I, too, like a touch of the dramatic!"

Holmes chortled again, though not as heartily as before.

"My apologies to all. I have been a little slow on the uptake, and to the lengths to which you have gone on my behalf ... all I can say is that the least I can do to repay your kindness, and especially that of brother Mycroft who has put aside his normal routine to travel here from the Diogenes Club, is to buy everybody the finest meal that Simpson's can provide."

"Green," said my wife.

"Green?" I queried, though Sherlock and Mycroft seemed to understand exactly what was inferred. It was Sherlock who was to reply.

"It will be my pleasure ... after our meal, I propose that make a stroll along the Strand and up to Regent Street, where in one of those fine establishments I suspect we will encounter a pair of green shoes that you will have had your eyes set upon for some little while."

This time we all looked at each other and laughed as one.

And Finally ...

when all is said and done and the end of the world is nigh and the Prince of Darkness assembles all his followers and asks for the 'real' Jack the Ripper to step forward and identify himself, those present will look on in astonishment and exclaim as one ...

"Who?"

Photographic
Appendix

All the photographs in this publication are by the author, or already in the public domain (www.commons.wikimedia.org). Particularly useful sources of illustrations include the Associated Newspapers Limited archive, and original publications such as *The Illustrated Police News*, *The Penny Illustrated Paper*, *Funny Folks Magazine*, *London Old & New*, and *Living London*. The various 1888 maps are based on those found at www.theundergroundmap.com.

[1] Dr. Thomas Neill Cream. [2] Montague John Druitt.
[3] Prince Albert Victor Christian Edward.
[4] Sir William Gull. [5] Assistant Chief Constable Melville
Macnaghten. [6] Assistant Commissioner Robert Anderson.
[7] James Maybrick. [8] Michael Ostrog. [9] Walter Sickert.

[10] Dr. Frances Tumblety. [11] Joseph Barnett.
[12] Buck's Row Board School. [13] The drop down to
Whitechapel station with the former Buck's Row Board
School behind. [14] The Working Lads Institute adjacent to
Whitechapel station. [15] The London Hospital.

[16] A typical street scene in the East End. [17] Inside a common lodging house in Spitalfields. [18] Moving day in the East End. [19] The daily queue of men looking for a day's work at the dock gates.

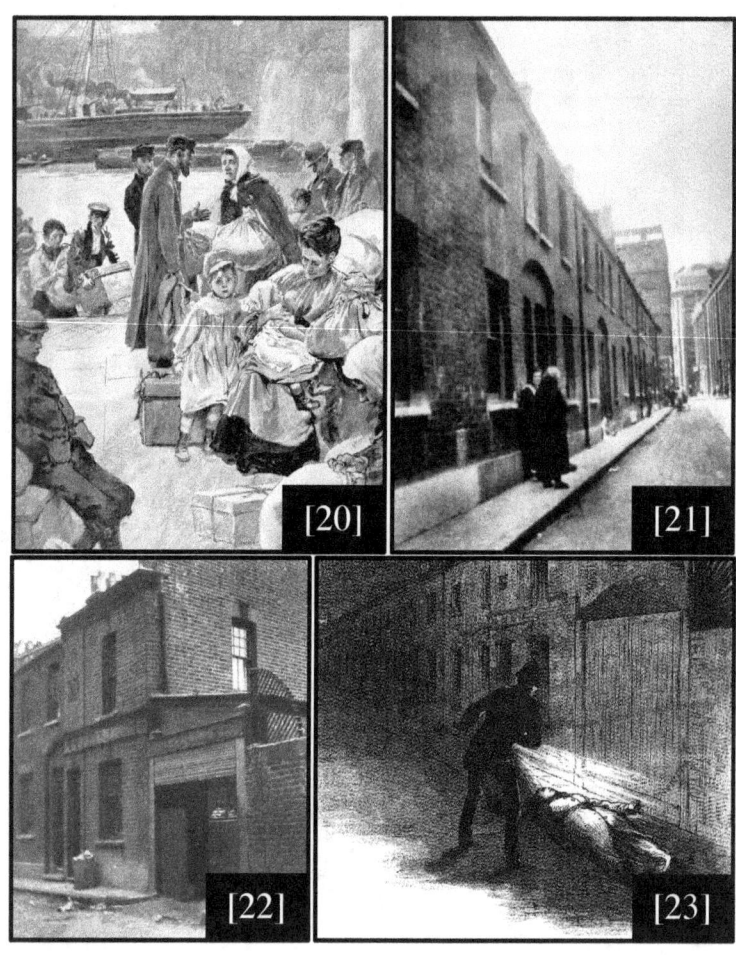

[20] Immigrants arriving in London at the turn of the 20th century. [21] Buck's Row with the board school in the distance. [22] The entrance to Brown's stable-yard where the body of Polly Nichols was found. [23] Press illustration of Police Constable John Neil finding the body of Polly Nichols.

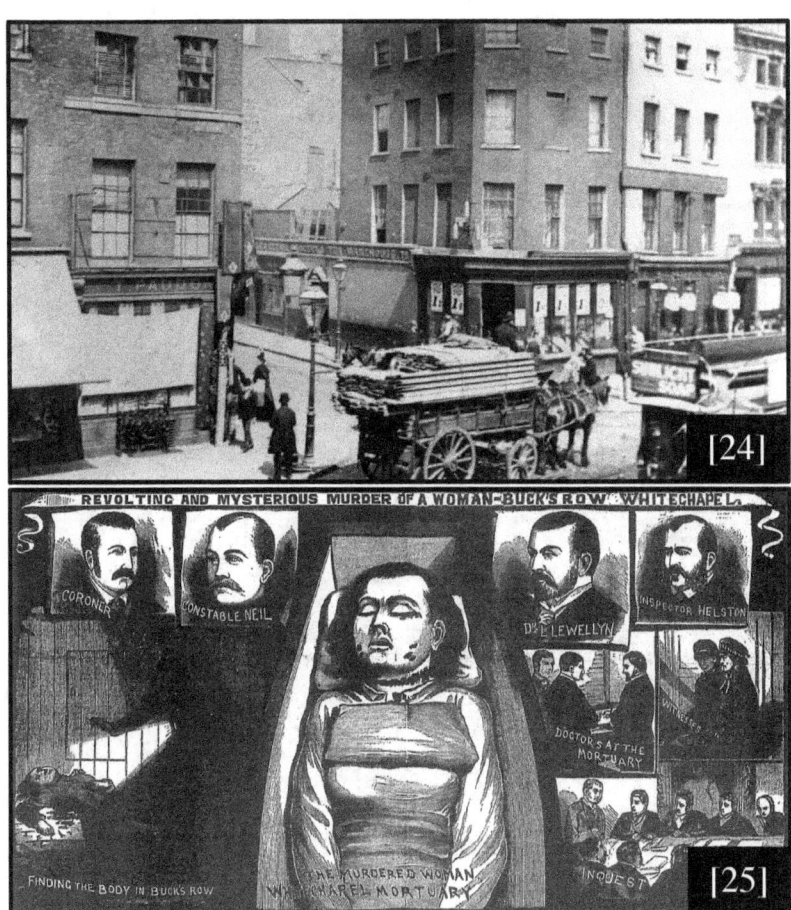

[24] The junction of Osborn Street and Whitechapel Road where Polly Nichols was last seen alive. [25] Coverage of the murder of Polly Nichols in *The Illustrated Police News*.

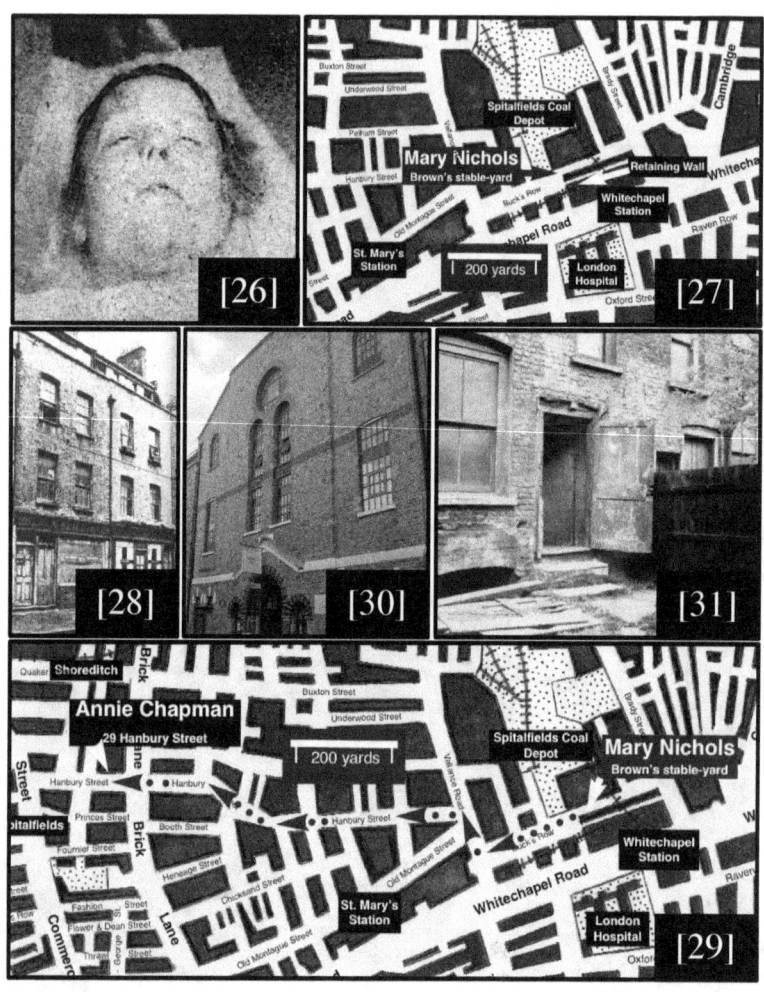

[26] Mortuary photograph of Polly Nichols. [27] Sketch map made by Holmes of the area where Polly Nichols was found. [28] Outside No. 29 Hanbury Street where the body of Annie Chapman was found in the back yard. [29] Sketch map made by Holmes showing the distance between the murder sites for Polly Nichols and Annie Chapman. [30] Hanbury Hall. [31] The rear of No. 29 Hanbury Street showing the exact spot that Annie Chapman's body was discovered.

[32] Mortuary photograph of Annie Chapman. [33] *The Illustrated Police News* coverage of the police investigation. [34] Chief Inspector Donald Swanson. [35] Metropolitan Police Commissioner Sir Charles Warren. [36] A 'Leather Apron' poster. [37] The 'Dear Boss' letter which was the first to use the epithet of Jack the Ripper.

[38] Sketch map by Holmes showing the possible exit routes from Hanbury Street. [39] Berner Street with the entrance to Dutfield's Yard being where the cart wheel is affixed to the wall. [40] Israel Schwartz observing the man who threw Elizabeth Stride to the ground. [41] Drawings from *The Illustrated Police News* concerning the Elizabeth Stride murder.

[42] Mortuary photograph of Elizabeth Stride. [43] Sketch
map by Holmes showing the location of the Commercial Road
goods yard with respect to where Elizabeth Stride's body was
found. [44] The main entrance to the Commercial Road goods
yard. [45] St. Botolph's church at Aldgate. [46] The corner in
Mitre Square where the corpse of Catherine Eddowes was
discovered.

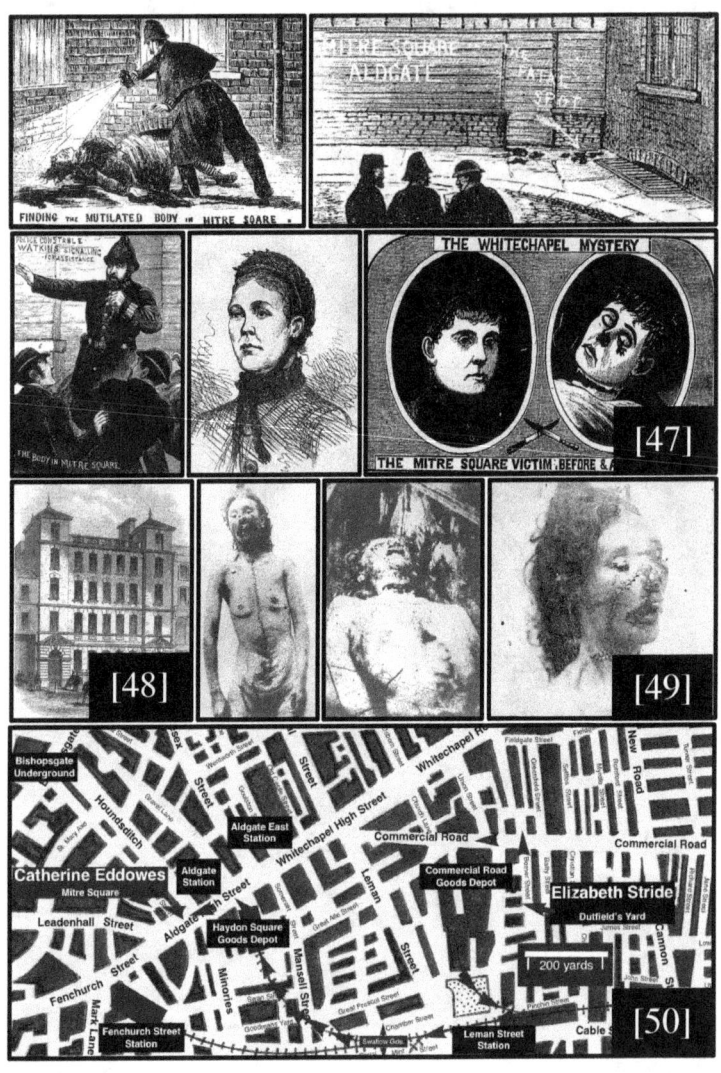

[47] Coverage in *The Illustrated Police News* of the murder of
Catherine Eddowes. [48] Bishopsgate police station.
[49] Three mortuary photographs of Catherine Eddowes.
[50] Sketch map by Holmes to show the route that the Ripper
might have taken to Mitre Square from Berner Street.

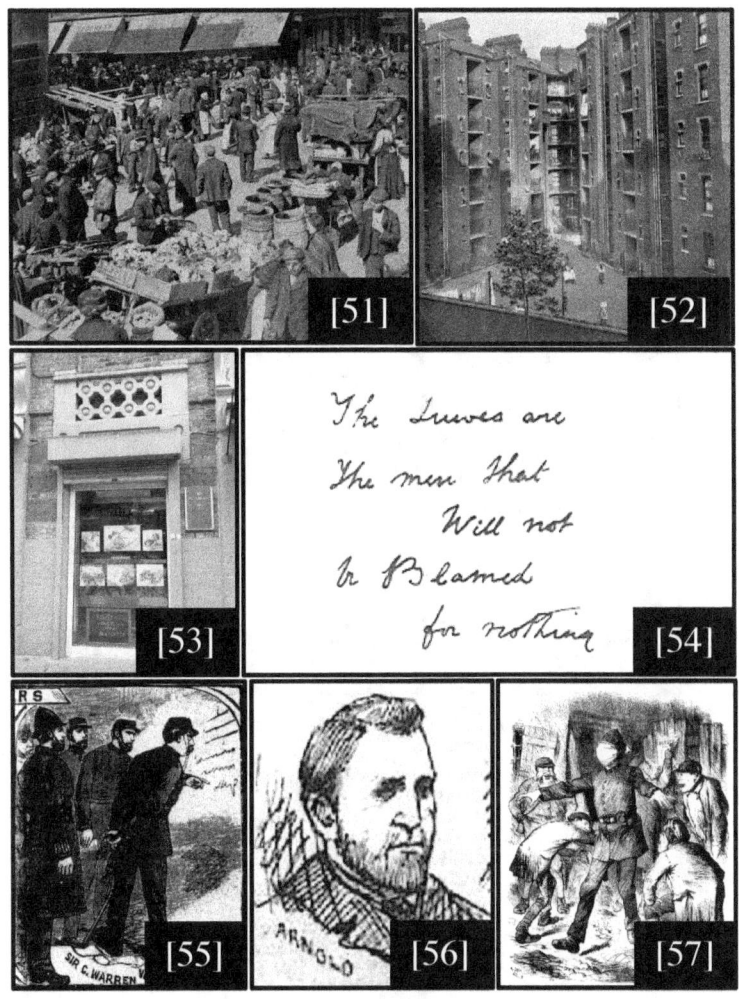

[51] Goulston Street on a busy Sunday morning. [52] A Model Dwelling block. [53] The entrance where the graffito was discovered. [54] A copy of the graffito as sent by Sir Charles Warren in a report to the Home Office. [55] Sir Charles Warren examining the graffito. [56] Police Superintendent Thomas Arnold. [57] Contemporary cartoon hinting at police incompetence as an officer plays 'blind man's buff' with the Ripper suspects.

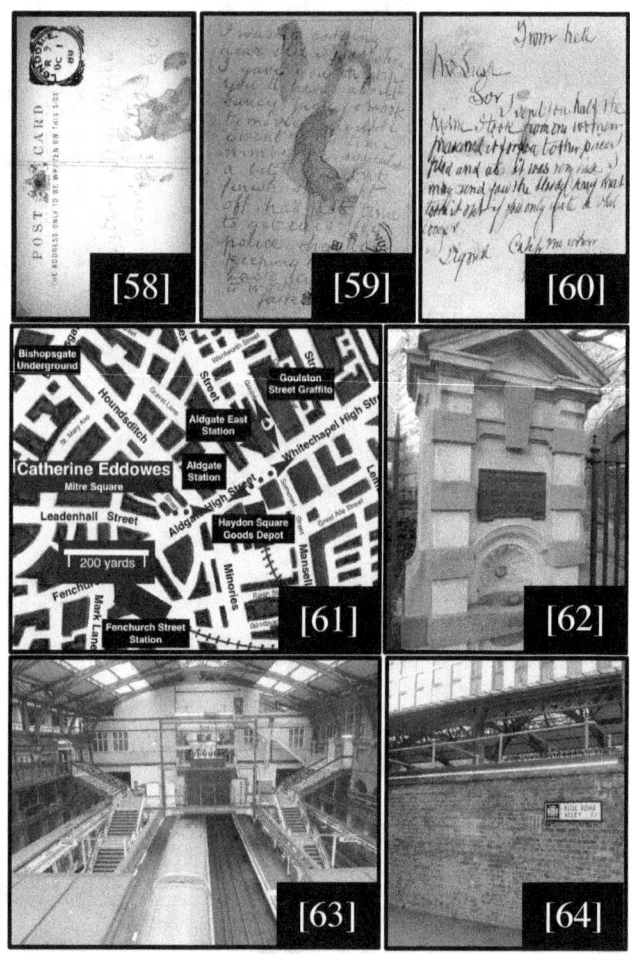

[58 & 59] The 'Saucy Jack' postcard. [60] The 'From Hell' letter. [61] Sketch map by Holmes of the possible route taken by the Ripper to Aldgate Underground station. [62] The water fountain outside St. Botolph's church. [63] Interior of Aldgate Underground station. [64] The modest wall to be scaled in Blue Boar Alley, the other side of which is the flat roof of the railway offices at Aldgate Underground station (see [65]).

[65] The station offices which abut Blue Boar Alley from which the tracks could be easily accessed. [66] Barnaby, Burgho, and another bloodhound on trial to assess their tracking abilities. [67] Another typical cartoon criticising the police efforts. [68] Mary Kelly's abode at No. 13 Miller's Court. [69] No. 26 Dorset Street showing the passageway entrance to Miller's Court. [70] Sketch map by Holmes showing the location of Mary Kelly's flat at Miller's Court.

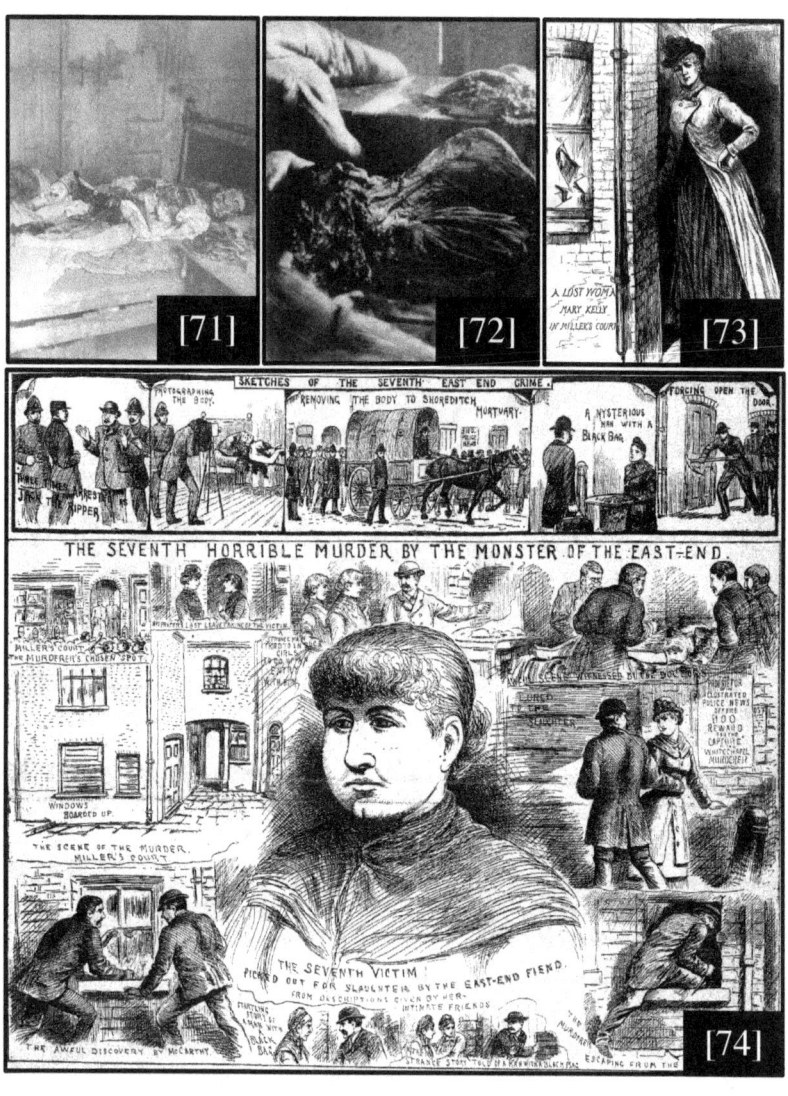

[71 & 72] Crime scene photographs taken of Mary Kelly.
[73] Mary Kelly. **[74]** Pictures from *The Illustrated Police News*
concerning the murder of Mary Kelly, who at the time was
regarded as the seventh victim of the Ripper.

[75] Detective Inspector Edmund Reid [76] Detective
Inspector Frederick Abberline. [77] Police Commissioner
James Monro. [78] The Providence Row night shelter with its
separate entrances for men and women guests. [79] White's
Row. [80] *The Illustrated Police News* drawings of the Ada
Wilson attack.

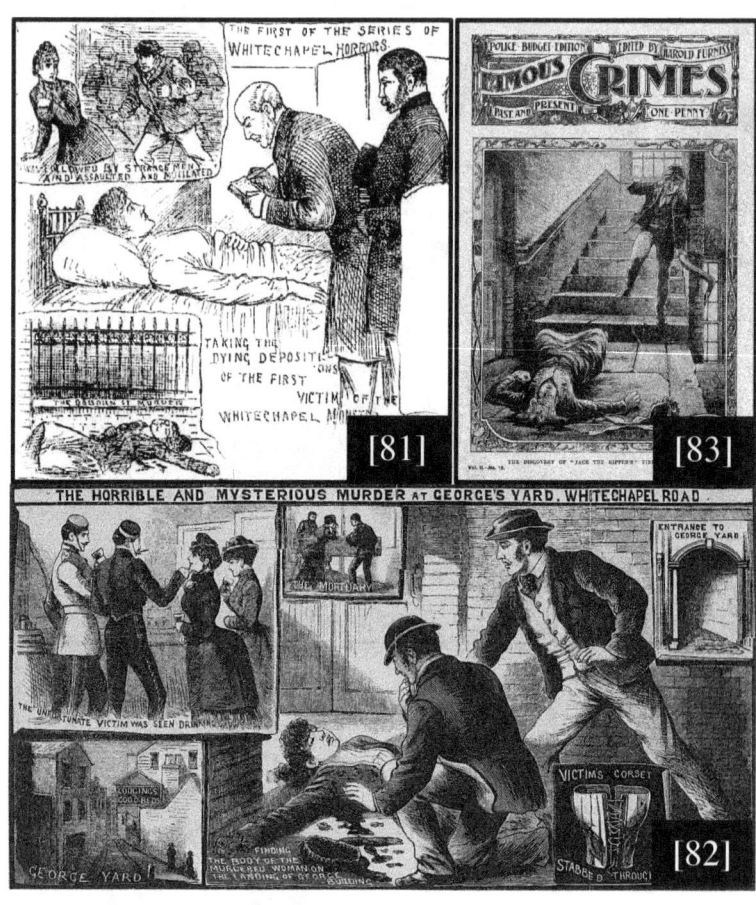

[81] *The Illustrated Police News* drawings of the murder of Emma Smith. [82] Drawings from *The Illustrated Police News* covering the murder of Martha Tabram. [83] 1903 cover from *Famous Crimes Past and Present* showing the discovery of Martha Tabram's body.

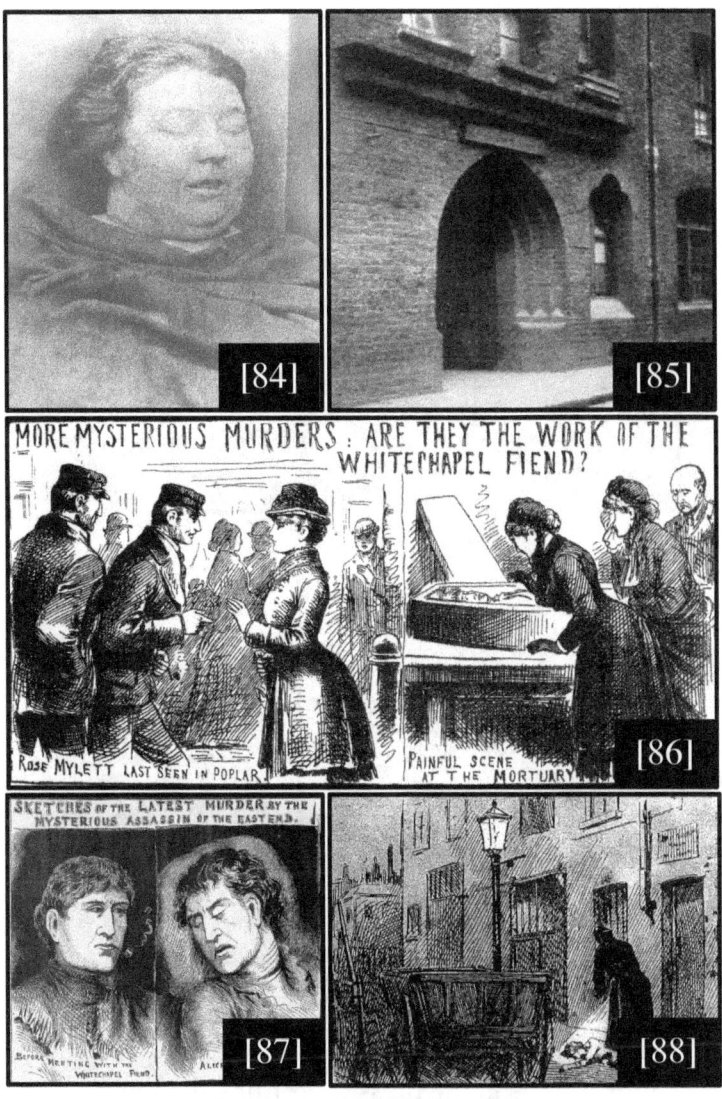

[84] Mortuary photograph of Martha Tabram. [85] Entrance to George Yard Buildings. [86] Drawings of the Catherine Mylett case as published in *The Illustrated Police News*. [87] Sketches of Alice McKenzie from *The Illustrated Police News*. [88] The discovery of Alice McKenzie's body by Police Constable Walter Andrews.

153

[89] Mortuary photograph of Alice McKenzie. **[90]** Illustrations in the press concerning the Pinchin Street torso. **[91]** *The Illustrated Police News* sketch for the Frances Coles murder.

[92] Mortuary photograph of Frances Coles.
[93] Railway plate layers at work. [94] Contemporary
photograph of two Underground trains passing each
other between Farringdon and Barbican stations.
The spur from the main line to the right originally
went under Smithfield market (one of the towers
of which can be seen in the background).

155

[95] The central aisle of the main building
at Smithfield market.

Acknowledgments

The author would like to thank **Roger Riccard**, Holmesian writer and friend who has written over fifty new Sherlock Holmes adventures, for his good advice and encouragement. A very special thanks must also go to **Lindsay Siviter**, renown crime historian and 'ripperologist' for her time in correcting all the factual errors (of which there were many) in the original manuscript.

References & Further Reading

When it comes to Jack the Ripper there is no shortage of books on the subject. The problem is that many contain factual errors, and are contradictory in nature – and this applies equally to those reports written at the time. It is hoped that this author has avoided the various pitfalls and presents here works that should belong to every 'Ripperologist', as well as those just interested in the history of London.

Jack the Ripper

Begg, Paul, *Jack the Ripper The Definitive History*, 310 pages, Pearson Education Limited, (2003), ISBN: 978-0-582506-31-2.

Clack, Robert & Hutchinson, Philip, *The London of Jack the Ripper Then and Now*, 190 pages, Breedon Books Publishing, (2007), ISBN: 978-1-859836-00-2.

Evans, Stuart P. & Rumbelow, Donald, *Jack the Ripper Scotland Yard Investigates*, 303 pages, Sutton Publishing, (2006), ISBN: 978-0-750942-28-7.

Evans, Stuart P. & Skinner, Keith, *The Ultimate Jack the Ripper Companion*, 758 pages, Carroll & Graf, (2000), ISBN: 978-0-786709-26-7.

Evans, Stuart P. & Skinner, Keith, *Jack the Ripper Letters From Hell*, 306 pages, Sutton Publishing, (2001), ISBN: 978-0-750925-49-5.

Evans, Stuart P. & Skinner, Keith, *Jack the Ripper and the Whitechapel Murders*, 12 pages, Public Record Office, (2002), ISBN: 978-1-903365-39-7.

Fido, Martin, *The Crimes, Detection & Death of Jack the Ripper*, 241 pages, Weidenfeld & Nicolson, ISBN: 978-0-297791-36-2.

Horsler, Val, *Jack the Ripper*, 112 pages, The National Archives, (2007), ISBN: 978-1-905615-14-8.

Rivett, Miriam & Whitehead, Mark, *Jack the Ripper*, 96 pages, Pocket Essentials, (2001), ISBN: 978-1-903047-69-9.

Sperati, J. P., *In the Footsteps of Jack the Ripper*, 207 pages, Irregular Special Press, (2021), ISBN: 978-1-901091-78-6.

Sugden, Philip, *The Complete History of Jack the Ripper*, 532 pages, Carroll & Graf, (1994), ISBN: 978-0-786709-32-8.

www.casebook.org – an excellent source of information on Jack the Ripper which also has links to the contemporary records.

www.jack-the-ripper.org – another excellent source of information on everything Jack the Ripper.

www.whitechapelsociety.com – website of The Whitechapel Society, a long-established historical society dedicated to studies of Jack the Ripper as well as wider aspects of Victorian and Edwardian east London.

London

Sims, George R., *Living London*, Volumes I-III, Cassell and Company, Limited, (1903).

Weinreb, Ben (Editor) & Hibbert, Christopher (Editor), *The London Encyclopaedia*, 1120 pages, MacMillan Reference, (2010), ISBN: 978-1-405049-25-2.

Walford, Edward, *Old and New London: A narrative of its History, its People, and its Places*, Volumes I-VI, Cassell & Company, Limited, (1902).

If you enjoyed this publication
you may also like …

Available in all good bookshops or direct
from the publisher at www.crime4u.com

"With five volumes you could fill that gap on that second shelf."
(Sherlock Holmes, *The Empty House*)

So why not complete your collection of murder mysteries from Baker Street Studios?
Available from all good bookshops, or direct from the publisher. To see full details of
all our publications, range of audio books, and special offers visit www.crime4u.com
where you can also join our mailing list.

MYSTERY OF A HANSOM CAB
SHERLOCK HOLMES AND DR. CRIPPEN
SHERLOCK HOLMES AND THE ABBEY SCHOOL MYSTERY
SHERLOCK HOLMES AND THE BAKER STREET DOZEN
SHERLOCK HOLMES AND THE BOLSHEVIK PLOT
SHERLOCK HOLMES AND THE BOULEVARD ASSASSIN
SHERLOCK HOLMES AND THE CASE OF THE HISSING SHAFT
SHERLOCK HOLMES AND THE CHARLIE CHAPLIN AFFAIR
SHERLOCK HOLMES AND THE CHILFORD RIPPER
SHERLOCK HOLMES AND THE CHINESE JUNK AFFAIR
SHERLOCK HOLMES AND THE CIRCUS OF FEAR
SHERLOCK HOLMES AND THE DISAPPEARING PRINCE
SHERLOCK HOLMES AND THE DISGRACED INSPECTOR
SHERLOCK HOLMES AND THE EGYPTIAN HALL ADVENTURE
SHERLOCK HOLMES AND THE FRIGHTENED CHAMBERMAID
SHERLOCK HOLMES AND THE FRIGHTENED GOLFER
SHERLOCK HOLMES AND THE GIANT'S HAND
SHERLOCK HOLMES AND THE GREYFRIARS SCHOOL MYSTERY
SHERLOCK HOLMES AND THE HAMMERFORD WILL
SHERLOCK HOLMES AND THE HILLDROP CRESCENT MYSTERY
SHERLOCK HOLMES AND THE HOLBORN EMPORIUM
SHERLOCK HOLMES AND THE HOUDINI BIRTHRIGHT
SHERLOCK HOLMES AND THE LONG ACRE VAMPIRE
SHERLOCK HOLMES AND THE MAN WHO LOST HIMSELF
SHERLOCK HOLMES AND THE MORPHINE GAMBIT
SHERLOCK HOLMES AND THE SANDRINGHAM HOUSE MYSTERY
SHERLOCK HOLMES AND THE SECRET MISSION
SHERLOCK HOLMES AND THE SECRET SEVEN
SHERLOCK HOLMES AND THE TANDRIDGE HALL MYSTERY
SHERLOCK HOLMES AND THE TELEPHONE MURDER MYSTERY
SHERLOCK HOLMES AND THE THEATRE OF DEATH
SHERLOCK HOLMES AND THE THREE POISONED PAWNS
SHERLOCK HOLMES AND THE TITANIC TRAGEDY
SHERLOCK HOLMES AND THE TOMB OF TERROR
SHERLOCK HOLMES AND THE YULE-TIDE MYSTERY
SHERLOCK HOLMES: A DUEL WITH THE DEVIL
SHERLOCK HOLMES AT THE RAFFLES HOTEL
SHERLOCK HOLMES AT THE VARIETIES
SHERLOCK HOLMES ON THE WESTERN FRONT
SHERLOCK HOLMES: THE GHOST OF BAKER STREET
SPECIAL COMMISSION
THE ADVENTURE OF THE SPANISH DRUMS
THE CASE OF THE MISSING STRADIVARIUS
THE ELEMENTARY CASES OF SHERLOCK HOLMES
THE TORMENT OF SHERLOCK HOLMES
THE TRAVELS OF SHERLOCK HOLMES
WATSON'S LAST CASE

Baker Street Studios Limited, Endeavour House, 170 Woodland Road,
Sawston, Cambridge CB22 3DX

www.ingramcontent.com/pod-product-compliance
Lightning Source LLC
Chambersburg PA
CBHW051243170626
46809CB00004B/1467